Taylor Flick

**The Three Circuits**

a study of the primary forces

Taylor Flick

**The Three Circuits**
*a study of the primary forces*

ISBN/EAN: 9783337780425

Printed in Europe, USA, Canada, Australia, Japan

Cover: Foto ©Andreas Hilbeck / pixelio.de

More available books at **www.hansebooks.com**

# THE THREE CIRCUITS:

## A STUDY OF

## THE PRIMARY FORCES.

### BY TAYLOR FLICK.

—— *And try to scan chaotic space,*
*Where everlasting forces work and weave*
*To build a home for men ; a place for things*
*Where order shall prevail.*

TO THE LOVERS OF SCIENCE

IN EVERY LAND

𝔗𝔥𝔦𝔰 𝔏𝔦𝔱𝔱𝔩𝔢 𝔙𝔬𝔩𝔲𝔪𝔢

IS RESPECTFULLY INSCRIBED.

# CONTENTS.

## CHAPTER I.

### THE REFLEX.

## CHAPTER II.

### WHAT IS MAGNETIC FORCE?

( v )

# CHAPTER III.

## WORLD FORMATION.

# CHAPTER IV.

## NIGHT-SIDE PHENOMENA.

# CHAPTER V.

## THE SOLAR ENIGMA.

# CHAPTER VI.

## SNOW CRYSTALS.

# CHAPTER VII.

## THE BEST EVIDENCE.

# PRELUDE.

## LOWER OCTAVE.

"One day, while Zadig, a Babylonian philosopher, was walking near a little wood, he saw hastening that way one of the queen's chief eunuchs, followed by a troop of officials who appeared to be in great anxiety, running hither and thither like men distraught in search of some lost treasure.

"'Young man,' cried the chief eunuch, 'have you seen the queen's dog?'

"Zadig answered modestly, 'A bitch, I think; not a dog.'

"'Quite right,' replied the eunuch.

"And Zadig continued: 'A very small spaniel, who has lately had puppies; she limps with the left foreleg, and has very long ears?'

"'Ah, you have seen her, then,' said the breathless eunuch.

"'No,' answered Zadig, 'I have not seen her, and I really was not aware that the queen possessed a spaniel.'

"By an odd coincidence, at the same time the handsomest horse in the king's stables broke away from his groom in the Babylonian plains. The grand huntsman and all his staff were seeking the horse with as much anxiety as the eunuch and his people the spaniel, and the grand huntsman asked Zadig if he had seen the king's horse go that way?

"'A first-rate galloper, small hoofed, five feet high, tail three feet and a-half long; cheek-pieces of the bit of twenty-three carat gold; shoes silver?' said Zadig.

"'Which way did he go? Where is he?' cried the grand huntsman.

"'I have not seen anything of the horse, and I never heard of him before,' replied Zadig.

"The grand huntsman and the chief eunuch made sure that Zadig had stolen both the king's horse and the queen's spaniel, so they haled him before the High court of Desterham, which at once condemned him to the knout and transportation for life to Siberia. But the sentence was hardly pronounced when the lost horse and spaniel were found. So the judges were under the painful necessity of reconsidering their decision, but they fined Zadig four hundred ounces of gold for saying he had seen that which he had not seen.

"The first thing was to pay the fine; afterward

Zadig was permitted to open his defense to the court, which he did, in the following terms :

" 'Stars of justice, abysses of knowledge, mirrors of truth, whose gravity is as that of lead, whose inflexibility is as that of iron, who rival the diamond in clearness, and possess no little affinity with gold ; since I am permitted to address your august assembly, I swear by Ormuzd, that I have never seen the respectable lady-dog of the queen, nor beheld the sacrosanct horse of the king of kings.'

"'' This is what happened. I was taking a walk toward the little wood, near which I subsequently had the honor to meet the venerable chief eunuch, and the most illustrious grand huntsman. I noticed the track of an animal in the sand, and it was easy to see that it was that of a small dog. Long faint streaks upon the little elevations of sand between the foot-marks, convinced me that it was a she-dog, with pendant dugs—showing that she must have had puppies not many days since. Other scrapings of the sand which always lay close to the marks of the fore-paws, indicated that she had very long ears ; and as the imprint of one foot was always fainter than those of the other three, I judged that the lady-dog of our august queen was, if I may venture to say so, a little lame.'

" 'With respect to the horse of the king of kings, permit me to observe that wandering through the paths which traverse the wood, I noticed the marks of horse shoes. They were all equidistant. 'Ah,' said I, 'This is a famous galloper.' In a narrow alley, only seven feet wide, the dust upon the trunks of the trees was a little disturbed at three feet and a-half from the middle of the path. 'This horse,' said I to myself, 'had a tail three feet and a-half long, and lashing it from one side to the other, he has swept away the dus:.' Branches of the trees met overhead at the height of five feet, and under them I saw newly fallen leaves; so I knew that the horse had brushed some of the branches, and was therefore five feet high. As to the bit, it must have been made of twenty-three carat gold, for he had rubbed it against a stone, which turned out to be a touchstone, with the properties of which I am familiar by experiment. Lastly, by the marks which his shoes made upon pebbles of another kind, I was led to think that his shoes were of fine silver.'

" All the judges admired Zadig's profound and subtle discernment, and the fame of it reached even the king and the queen. From the ante-rooms to the presence-chamber, Zadig's name was in everybody's mouth; and although many of the magi were of the opinion that he ought to be burned as a sorcerer, the king commanded that the four hundred ounces of gold which he had been fined should be restored to him, so the officers of the court went in state with the four hundred ounces; only they retained three hundred and ninety-eight for legal expenses and their servants expected fees."

---

# PRELUDE.

---

## MIDDLE OCTAVE.

"SHALL the mole from his night underground
Call the beasts of the day-glare to flee ;
Shall the owl charge the birds : 'I am wise
Go to ! Seek the shadows with me !'
Shall a man bind his eyes and exclaim ;
'It is vain that men weary to see?'

"Let him walk in the gloom whoso will,
Peace be with him ! But whence is his right
To assert that the world is in darkness
Because he has turned from the light?
Or to seek to o'ershadow my day
With the pall of his self-chosen night?

"I have listened like David's great son ;
To the voice of the beast and the bird ;
To the voice of the trees and the grass.—
Yea a voice from the stones I have heard ;
And the sun and the moon and the stars
In their courses re-echo the word !

" And one word speak the bird and the beast,
And the hyssop that springs in the wall,
And the cedar that lifts its proud head
Upon Lebanon stately and tall
And the rocks and the sea and the stars :—
And know is the message of all.

" For the answer has ever been nigh
Unto him who would question and learn ;
How to bring the stars near to his gaze ;—
In what orbits the planets must turn ;—
Why the apple must fall from the bough ;—
What fuel the sun-fires burn.

" Whence came life ?  In the rocks is it writ,
And no finger hath graven it there ?
Whence came light ?  Did its motions arise
Without bidding ?  Will science declare
That the law ruling all hath upsprung
From no mind that abideth nowhere ?

" ' Yea I know !' cried the true man of old
And whosoe'er wills it may know
My redeemer existeth I seek

For a sign of his presence and lo
As he spoke to the light and it was ;
So he speaks to my soul and I know !''
—SOLOMON SOLIS COHEN, *in the Century Magazine.*

# PRELUDE.

## UPPER OCTAVE.

THE heavens declare the glory of God: and the firmament showeth his handy work.

2. Day unto day uttereth speech, and night unto night showeth knowledge.

3. *There is* no speech nor language *where* their voice is not heard.

4. Their line is gone out through all the earth, and their words to the end of the world. In them hath he set a tabernacle for the sun ;

5. Which *is* as a bridegroom coming out of his chamber, *and* rejoiceth as a strong man to run a race.

6. His going forth *is* from the end of the heaven, and his circuit unto the ends of it: and there is nothing hid from the heat thereof.

7. The law of the LORD *is* perfect, converting the soul : the testimony of the LORD *is* sure, making wise the simple :

8. The statutes of the LORD *are* right, rejoicing the heart :

the commandment of the LORD *is* pure, enlightening the eyes :

9. The fear of the LORD *is* clean, enduring for ever : the judgments of the LORD *are* true *and* righteous altogether.

10. More to be desired *are they* than gold, yea, than much fine gold ; sweeter also than honey and the honey-comb.

11. Moreover, by them is thy servant warned : *and* in keeping of them *there is* great reward.

12. Who can understand *his* errors ? cleanse thou me from secret *faults.*

13. Keep back thy servant also from presumptuous *sins ;* let them not have dominion over me : then shall I be upright, and I shall be innocent from the great transgression.

14. Let the words of my mouth, and the meditation of my heart, be acceptable in thy sight, O LORD, my strength and my redeemer.

# THE THREE CIRCUITS.

## CHAPTER I.

### THE REFLEX.

In the year 1874 I lived in one of the new towns in southwestern Kansas. My residence was what might be called a substantially built suburban farm-house; I also had an office in town, for by the way I am a lawyer.

The country thereabout, at the time mentioned, was very sparsely settled. Indeed, the town would not have been called a town anywhere except in the West, where promises and possibilities were, at least in those days, often accepted as if they were things *in esse* and *in presenti.*

You may infer that my practice was at the minimum. Indeed, I will admit that at the time referred to, I had not a single client. But as I owned my cottage and office and enjoyed a small income derived from outside sources I never really wanted for

anything, and at times I flattered myself that I was
of a contented disposition as to worldly affairs.

I will mention here, that besides my law library,
I was happy in the possession of a small collection
of miscellaneous books, and with these I spent the
greater part of my leisure.

But, as time passed, I became somewhat discon-
tented, and then I conceived the idea that I was by
nature fitted for a more exalted calling.   And shortly
thereafter I foolishly concluded that I was a philosopher, or at least an amateur.

At this period I commenced writing a treatise the
title of which was, as nearly as I can recollect, "The
Composition of Light and Heat as shown by the Coin-
cidences of Natural Phenomena."

The subject seemed to me at that time to be broad
enough to serve as a basis for quite a work, and I
may say that my opinion in that respect has not been
changed since.

I suppose I had written nearly one hundred pages
and collected a large number of valuable quotations,
when I began to perceive that my subject was spread-
ing out, as it were, in arithmetical ratio, and that it
was also becoming more and more complex in all its
bearings.

Also I discovered about the same time, that constantly thinking and writing on the same subject, had developed within me a fierce thirst to master the problems that were gathering around me thick and fast. And so I struggled from day to day to wrest the secrets of nature from nature itself. As a result of this, I found that abstracted moods were growing on me, and in these I often thought I would give all that I possessed to master the work I had set out to do.

One morning in June I had, without realizing it, passed into one of these reveries, and was trying to imagine how the sun had been enabled to keep up its supply of heat during all the ages, notwithstanding the enormous quantities radiated to the earth and planets and throughout infinite space; when my attention was attracted, and there stepped in at the open door a reverend looking old gentleman, clothed in a velvet coat, knee-breeches and hose. Being a little surprised, I only noticed his dress in a cursory manner, but I distinctly remember that he had a sword at his side.

As soon as he saw that I recognized his entrance, he bowed profoundly and slightly retreating as he recovered, said, " I have been told that you are a philosopher? "

" I am not," I replied, " but you may consider that I am an amateur."

" I am the spirit," said he, " of a gentleman and a philosopher of the tenth century. I am the author of several important works. I hope, sir, you have read my work on Astrology, and also a treatise of mine setting forth in full my reasons for believing that persons born under certain signs of the zodiac and other peculiar conditions therein mentioned, might be able, by following my directions, to discover a stone that would turn everything touched by it into gold."

"I have not had the honor," I replied. " But I am as glad to see you as if I had read your works. Have a seat and try one of my cigars."

" Sir," he said, with some severity, " I consider it beneath a man in my station to indulge in idle practices or pleasures whichever this may be."

" Then, sir, what may be the object of your call ? "

" I have been permitted to revisit the earth in answer to a longing I had to know what progress had been made in philosophy since I left it. I have seen your railroads, steamships, telegraph and telephone lines, and I think they are useful inventions. But I would take a deeper interest in them if they were in my line."

" Beg pardon," I said, " will you inform me what is your line ? "

" Well, sir, I take a deep interest in all scientific subjects."

" What is it you would deem a scientific subject ? "

" I consider Mathematics an almost exact science ; Astronomy, Astrology and Physics are sciences. There may be others."

" Then," I said, " I have the honor to inform you that our people hold that these inventions are in the line of physics."

He seemed perplexed but made no reply. Addressing him, I asked, " Is there any particular subject you would prefer to talk about? "

" I would like you to explain this new idea that the earth is a globe, and that it is upheld by nothing. And if it be so, which I do not believe, then why I and other eminent philosophers did not discover the fact."

" I will state the evidence," I answered, " which I can promise you amounts to a demonstration, and then you may be able to find the reason yourself. The most convincing proof lies in the fact that mariners have sailed all around it."

" Well, sir, if such grave matters can be settled in the minds of your people by the tales of mariners, I might as well go my way, for I never pay any attention to sailors' yarns."

"But my dear sir, it is not their tales, but the actual courses and distances as shown by the compass and the log."

"Oh, your compass may be all right and so may the log, whatever that may be, but were they not in the hands of men who have always been noted for telling stories that nobody could believe?"

"Then, as further proof, I will inform you that our architects and mechanics find in erecting tall buildings, that with the most careful plumbing, the outside walls recede from each other, and allowance is usually made to correct the angular spread caused by the earth's sphericity."

"Then I know," he replied, "that your architects have been imposed upon. And to such a mechanic I would say, if you handle your plumb-line so carelessly that your walls become farther separated, you had better be serving as an apprentice or at work as a journeyman. Sir," he added, "I came to you to hear the explanation of a philosopher. I know to a certainty that if this earth were a spherical body, all the water would be emptied out of it. And that is reason enough for me if there were no others."

"Then, if you know this," I said, "you are not in condition to receive any light on the subject, and the remainder of your question is answered already."

He bowed very stiffly and bidding me " Fare-well," left the office, closing the door after him.

I thought how hard it seems to be for one to gain knowledge contrary to that which he has learned from the books. And especially when he is vain, and flatters himself that he knows all about it. That old philosopher will believe from now to the end of time that the earth is flat and that the limits of the sea surrounding it can never be known. And he may even go further and think that no inquiry about it ought to be made.

Just as my thoughts turned again to the solar problem, the door opened, and there was another caller. He was a fine looking young man, apparently of quiet deportment; he walked straight to where I sat and lifting his hat in urbane style, said :

" Are you a philosopher ? "

' " I am not a philosopher," I replied, " but an ama-teur."

" I am a reflex," he said.

" What ? "

" I am the reflex."

" Well, sir ! " I said, " Will you have the kind-ness to inform me, what a reflex is, and how you came to be one ? "

" I am the reflex," he replied, " of a lover of science

who will live on the earth about the middle of the twentieth century; I have been permitted to come to you and explain as far as I can the scientific problems that have been troubling your mind."

" My friend," I said, " No one can ever know how glad I am to see you ; have a seat and smoke." Handing him the best cigar I had.

He declined the offer, and in a reflective manner said :

" What is it you would like to know ? "

" I can hardly tell you," I replied. " I find that I have by hard work pushed myself into a maze of difficulties; that the work I am writing is leading me into all the sciences, that infinite phenomena lead to infinite experiment and these to infinite conclusions. And so I have lost my way and my work is stopped."

" Cheer up ! " he said smilingly, " I think I know what is the trouble with your work. In the first place, you have set yourself the task of conceiving as fully as if it were a single proposition, all the knowledge the human race has acquired in two, perhaps in three sciences, and of placing it before your readers so that they will comprehend it at a glance. You then intend to point out what part of it is in accord with observed phenomena and what is not. After which you intend to offer certain hypotheses which you conceive to be true, and show that they also will account for the same phenomena as in the first instance, and that in addition thereto they will throw new light on various phenomena which have hitherto remained wholly unexplained."

" That is about it," I said.

" Then," he replied, " I feel bound to tell you and I hope I do so kindly. I really do not think you are able to undertake such a work."

" Then I had better abandon the whole subject at once ; indeed, I was about to do so before you came in."

" No,—in the second place you have fallen into the same error that hampered the mind of the old philosopher who just left you. You have too much confidence in the learning contained in scientific works and altogether too much in speculations that have by accident crept into school books." Then pausing a moment, he added : " It behooves you, as well as him, to look more to nature and up to Him, who is the creator of all. In short, that you divest yourself of every prejudice, and with the knowledge you have derived from the books, present yourself, as it were, a sheet of white paper, to receive whatsoever your God may desire to write thereon."

After which he called my attention to the fact that

all the heavenly bodies are moving in elliptical orbits. The inference he drew from it was that planetary motion being in curvature, left no reason for us to think that primary force ever acted in right lines.

He advanced the idea that the body of the sun is as cool as that of the earth; that there might be zones on its surface favored with a fine climate, and perhaps, great rivers and mountains there. He suggested the possibility that its polar regions are as cold as ours. Moreover, he claimed that its light was not the effect of incandescence, or its heat the result of either combustion or friction.

At the end of a couple of hours, which had been very interesting ones to me, he bade me "Good-bye," saying he would call again in the morning.

What a degree of excellence, I thought, that young man has attained; how easy his manner; with what grace he tempers that which would otherwise be offensive; I will cultivate his acquaintance; his friendship may be worth having.

The next day we strolled out on the plains which he had never before seen.

"I am surprised," said he, "that there is so little grass, and what is stranger still the ground is almost covered with bones. As far as the eye can reach I see everywhere heads and limbs and whole skeletons."

"The grass," I replied, "is called buffalo grass after
the name of the wild cattle that roam over the plains.
It is always short, even in the middle of summer, but
it is very nutritious, and is said to be about as good
grazing in winter as in summer. The bones are those
of the buffalo; they lie just as you see them for
hundreds of miles; in fact, throughout the whole
western plateau, which is yet tolerably well filled
with the living animals; but hunters in great numbers are after them all the time. Some hunt them
merely for sport, others make a business of it; selling
their hides in the towns."

"It appears to me," he said, "that the sky is a
deeper blue than I have seen elsewhere, and that it
maintains its full color to the ground line; and I
either imagine it," he added, "or it is really the
bluest and loveliest I have ever seen."

It pleased me to hear the country praised and so I
remarked:

"You will find, if you conclude to settle here, that
the air is pure and invigorating. Owing to the altitude of the country there is no malaria in the atmosphere, but a large quantity of ozone which is said to
be beneficial to invalids. Ladies of delicate consti-
tutions often sleep here with their chamber windows
open."

"I have heard that the country is infested with villains who make life and property insecure."

"The fact," I replied, "may be generally admitted and yet it needs to be explained. You must know that native or domestic cattle are abundant in this country, and that they run at large and subsist by grazing both in summer and in winter. This manner of life has made them nearly as wild as the buffalo. Indeed, at times the former are more dangerous than the latter. The young men who take charge of the cattle are called cow-boys; the cow-boy is not a villain in any sense, but simply a bold, self-reliant blusterer; however, they go armed with large revolvers which they sometimes need for defence.

"There is another class of men who arm themselves in the same style; their disposition is more quiet than that of the cow-boy; they are inclined to say little and do a great deal of harm; they hang around railroad towns, where Texas cattle arrive in droves and are shipped to market. They are desperadoes and true villains; the liquor saloon is their home and gambling their profession. They prey on the cow-boys and foolish young men and old ones, too, from all parts of the country; they are all desperate men, some of them horse thieves and railroad train robbers. They delight in calling themselves such names as

Wild Bill, Cherokee Dan, Buckskin Joe, etc. In saloon broils they are killing each other all the time, and take pride in boasting that they 'intend to be buried with their boots on;' when two or three of them are killed in a night many persons consider it a fortunate circumstance ; they are unpleasant men to deal with, but generally not dangerous to good citizens."

"What a dreadful phase of human life ! " he said.

"They have developed or degenerated, whichever you please to call it, from the inexperienced young man through the cow-boy state into murderers."

"It is a pity," he replied, "that Darwin had not known this and cited them as an example of retrogression."

After I had explained the condition of the country as it then was, we spent the remainder of the day talking of the general affairs then current, and at the close of it we were friends and he became our guest.

He was an enthusiastic amateur and, I think, a good scholar. He never tired of observing the clouds or of noting the direction of the wind, and it always pleased him to talk about such phenomena as the country afforded. And so we became fast friends and scoured the country together on foot and on horse-back ; I loved to call him Flex, and I took no pleasure in rambling unless he was with me. We enjoyed our home, too, notwithstanding the trouble that came afterwards.

Many a summer evening we sat on the veranda and watched the sun clip the horizon without the slightest diminution of its mid-day splendor. At such times the air was so exceedingly dry that a wet handkerchief would dry in about the time it takes to write the fact; and buffalo meat hung in the sun would soon cure into excellent dried beef.

One afternoon we sat there with our feet on the railing enjoying ourselves to the utmost. Flex was in fine vein; he kept talking in a low voice about the tides and what caused them; and from that he began to explain aerial tides and " highs " and " lows " and " frost line tables," and thermometers that never reach the highest or lowest degree; and " latitudinal belts," whatever they may be. However, I do know that he made it all very satisfactory to me, and I said, " I believe you are very nearly right about the matter."

Looking up we discovered a cloud in the west; I do not believe it rose or came from anywhere; I think it formed just where it was; but that would not have been remarkable had it not acted so strangely. It was not an angry-looking cloud, but it shrunk up

and spread out again, and while we looked at it other
clouds formed and drifted rapidly toward it. This
process continued and when night came on it filled
the whole northwestern part of the heavens; it then
had a beautiful greenish appearance, and we could
hear the muttering thunder and see the zigzag lightning. All this time there was a very slight breeze
toward the storm which was apparently moving
toward us. Just after dark the wind lulled and for
a few minutes there was a dead calm; such a calm
as only a poet can describe.

> "Deep watery clouds o'erspread the sky,
>     Dead stillness reigns in air;
> There is not even a breeze on high
>     The gossamer to bear.

> "The woods are hushed, the waters rest,
>     The lake is dark and still;
> Reflecting on its shadowy breast
>     Each form of rock and hill."

In this profound silence we heard a blow strike the
roof of the house as if it were delivered with an axe,
then suddenly there came a burst of wind from the
northwest; roaring it came and seemingly striking
all the four sides of the house at once, it shook it
from top to bottom. Instantly the rain fell in tor-

rents and masses of hailstones came pounding along breaking glass and sash and adding to an uproar that was already appalling. Meanwhile the lightning had gathered itself into an electrical display that filled the whole firmament; the thunder rolled continuously, while the howling hurricane, loaded with ice, swept through the house, and strained, and tugged, and wrestled with it as if determined to destroy it, and still the brave house stood. The veranda went with the first blast, the window blinds were torn to fragments and carried away; the lighter furniture followed; the floors were half shoe top deep in water and ice and broken glass, and while rivers of water still came pouring down the fearful storm passed on. And we, utterly dismayed at the wild work of the elements, thanked God that we were still alive and that the almost ruined structure still stood over us.

The next morning we found that everything except ourselves had been blown from the premises; the greater part of our household property lie strewed in the wake of the storm. The grain that stood ripening the day before was pounded to the earth, ground to powder and blown away. The grass and weeds had left by the same route; by noon the hot sun made the outlook as brown as a stubble field in winter.

After this we had fine weather for several weeks, and Flex and I determined to take a trip and see what was transpiring on the plains, where buffalo hunters were holding high carnival, if such it might be called, where one party had all profit and the other was invariably the victim.

We soon procured a covered wagon, team of horses, provisions, cooking outfit, etc., and one bright morning we bid good-bye to our friends and " pulled out for the front."

I think I never will enjoy anything like I did that trip. The weather was delightful. Crossing the Arkansas river with some difficulty, we took our course southwest by west, intending to strike the range in about sixty miles in that direction.

The country we passed over was very high-rolling prairie, without any streams of water. We saw no buffalo that day, but wolves were numerous, and antelopes scampered from every rise of ground.

As the hours passed on, we could notice that we were getting nearer to the range by the buffalo paths that began to cross each other at sharp angles in the direction of lower land that lay far ahead. Now and then a lighter path showed where the calves had trotted alongside their mothers. The bones of the slain literally covered the ground.

Toward evening we arrived at a small stream, and went into camp pretty well tired out, not having seen a road that day, except a dim one that we crossed early in the morning.

There was no wood at the place we camped, but we gathered a few "chips," which, by the way, make a very good fire, made some good coffee, ate our suppers with a relish, and slept as soundly in the wagon as if we had been on feather-beds.

The next morning we broke camp early, resolved to reach the range that night if possible.

The country we passed over was not different from that we had seen the day before. By noon it became very monotonous, and conversation ceased in a great measure for the want of new subjects.

But Flex was not to be discouraged. He kept my spirits up talking about Polar axes, magnetic poles, circuits of pure force, infinite areas in space, and solar systems far away from ours. Sometimes I thought his mind was not on the earth, but soaring on angel's wings throughout the universe.

Antelope became very numerous; large herds of them in sight all the time; and wolves snarled and growled at us as we passed by.

Toward evening we began to see " bunches of buffalo," sometimes fifty or more, and one herd that we estimated at three hundred. And later we camped on a small stream that we thought might be the head of the Beaver or Pala Dora creek.

We rested very comfortably that night, although the wolves howled dreadfully.

The next morning we were awakened by the crack of rifles, and we soon learned that we were among the hunters on the eastern edge of the great southern herd.

The hunters are usually divided into companies of four or eight men, who are partners, or, as they say, "in cahoots."

Their work is a bloody one. They are armed with breech-loading rifles of very heavy calibre. They organize themselves with special reference to the habits of the animals. They have learned that a hunter can, by using care and patience, crawl into the centre of a great herd, say a thousand or more. Having secured this situation, he has the advantage of short rifle-range, and can kill them at will. Just as long as one drops dead at every shot, there will be little or no disturbance. Sometimes a few of the nearest will throw up their heads, and perhaps one or two of them will snort, but in a few minutes they will resume feeding. But when one is wounded, it will run bellowing away, followed by the whole herd, and they may not stop for several miles. Now, when the skinning begins, it is a saving of time and labor to have the dead lying near together. For this reason the best marksman is selected to do the shooting.

We were not hunters, not even sportsmen; Captain Custard, the leader of one of the companies, informed us as to their methods. He said that he had often "downed" from twenty-five to thirty before he had the misfortune to wound one.

The next year the same informant stated that he believed that four-fifths of the whole race were killed in the year 1874.

We visited several of the camps and found the hunters generally brave, good-hearted, hospitable frontiersmen. After which we went to the salt-fields in the Indian territory and from thence home.

Shortly after this trip came the grasshopper; how he learned that the cup of our joy was again filling up no one can tell; it is not likely that he read any of the glowing circulars that had been sent abroad, nor that any of his people had preceded him and written about the salaries of county officers; he probably took counsel of his stomach, and thereupon called an assembly by nations and by families, and doubtless all were chosen. And then, with an unanimity never before equalled, every grasshopper, without respect to previous condition, broke up house-keeping and straightway emigrated to Kansas.

It was a bright morning late in July; the van-guard arrived in clouds about ten o'clock; by noon, they filled the air as if all the sands of the seashore had been instantly turned into grasshoppers; they flew so thickly that the sky had a dark-brown appear-ance. The earth was also covered with them through-out scores of counties. All the windows and doors had to be closed to exclude them, and there was a continual clatter as they drifted against the sides of the building. Domestic fowls were overwhelmed with delight; they stood at such places with open mouths upturned to receive them; the stomach of a chicken in grasshopper time can be compared to noth-ing except a bottomless reservoir.

The appetite of the hoppers was boundless; they hesitated not but pounced upon all that the hail had here and there left, and in less than two days they harvested and stored in their greedy stomachs all the remainder of the crop of 1874. After which they prowled around a day or two as if to make sure that the job was well done and then they left as suddenly as they came.

That was a long to be remembered year in the annals of western Kansas; evidently the country was ruined. Oh! you may well believe, it is hard times when farmers stare at each other and ask: "Where is bread?" But it was long ago, and it seems to me now like a horrid nightmare of the past.

As the fall passed on large-hearted men and women learned of our wants, and after all the bread came, and the winter went by without more suffering than we were able to bear.

During the year 1875, our home life differed but little from what it had been. My law library increased and also my practice in the courts, but not enough to prevent Flex and I from continuing our investigations. We lost no opportunity to visit the country, but at this time the settlement had extended so much that we generally rode horseback.

I think every professional man ought to keep a horse or two, and then with such a friend as I had to accompany him, he should be supremely happy; at least I was.

We made long trips, tethered our horses and walked to the nearer hills.

Once we sat on two huge skeleton heads, far out on the plains; it was a fine Indian summer afternoon, early in November, 1876. We were on a high divide overlooking the valley of the Walnut; the bluffs and headlands that marked its course could be seen for miles. In the opposite direction the Buckner wended its way in sight and not more than four or five miles away. A light blue smoke or haze lay between, but not enough to prevent us from seeing the thin fringe of cotton-wood trees and brush that here and there lined its banks; now and then, with a glass we could see a dark animal or two saunter down its bank apparently to drink ; my enjoyment of the scenery was complete; after while, Flex said, " Why don't you write a cosmology ? "

" Do you mean me ? "

" Yes, I think you could do it," he replied. I was surprised that he should make such a remark, since he knew my want of knowledge of the subject, and that my practice was increasing. However, after reflecting a moment I said :

"Don't you think it wrong to dabble in such matters ? "

" No indeed," he replied, "I think much good would follow it, because the ideas of thoughtful men lead to experiment and there are many learned men who devote their lives to that work. It has been said that the announcement of Newton's theory, and the revival of discussion that followed it doubled the world's knowledge in a few years. In the second place, a monstrous theory has been accepted, or, at least, if it has not been accepted it has been treated as if it were true, and the result is, that astronomy is having grafted on it a literature of white-hot suns and red-hot planets. As if God were unable to light and warm his worlds without making the finest of them useless camp-fires. This fiery hypothesis is of an age when men began to learn that a great force could be obtained from the expansion and contraction of matter when subjected to different temperatures. Its hold on the public mind has been strengthened by the practical illustration of steam as a working power; in this way the conclusion has become established, that God created the worlds by the expansive power of heat, and that He lights and warms the earth by solar heat resulting from combustion or frictional collision. It hardly needs to be said that the worlds so employed are good for nothing else. Moreover it is a clumsy plan, and not in accord with the wisdom of him who has all power at his command. It has taught us to think that a third-rate manifestation is the primary force in nature, and so we have been led into difficulties from which there is no escape without making a complete radical change of base."

"I think you are right about this," I said.

Continuing, he said: "Such a work ought to

breathe a spirit of love to God and love to men and kindness to every creature."

He finished by saying: "I believe He intends that we should pry into His works, and so gain more knowledge of His omnipotence."

"Well, really," I replied; "You have lost sight of your own inconsistency. You first say that I ought to write it, and then you raise the standard on high, forgetting that I am a western lawyer. Flex, I suppose I am honest as the world goes; that is to say, I would not steal—a pin."

He interrupted me, laughing, "What if it were the estate of a deceased millionaire?"

"Oh, that alters the case. If he had been a client of mine, I would have advised him to spend nine-tenths of it in relieving distress. You and I have seen some. Now, if some benevolent lawyer has the cash, I think that millionaire's ghost is served about right."

The afternoon was one of the finest; there was not a breath of wind, and the air was delicious. Now and then we could hear the crack of a rifle, and then two or three dark-colored beasts would hurry across some neighboring hill, reminding us that the monarchs of the plains were still going down. Then I began to think of the wide-spread extermination of

these gentle creatures; that not one in a thousand of
them ever turned on his tormentors.  I thought of
the short, sweet grass, as good in winter as in summer, and that cold rains seldom or never occurred at
any season of the year.  On the whole, it seemed to
me that the country was well adapted to their wants
in every respect.  Then I said : " Flex, I think this
whole business is an outrage."

"We were speaking of God's works," he replied.

"But I am speaking of the ruthless, wanton destruction of an entire race of creatures.  I was thinking how they had lived here all their lives, and drank
at every stream of water for hundreds of years.  I
tell you I believe the land is theirs; that they own
it in fee simple.  Their great brown mouths have
kissed every acre of it more than a thousand times.
I believe the trouble and misery we have endured is
a just punishment for such a wide-spread, cruel,
wicked act."  Pausing for breath, I added : " The
government ought to be ashamed of itself."

"Our government," he quietly remarked, " can
express no measure of shame or indignation except
such as may be in the minds of the individuals that
compose it."  And then, with a smile, added : "You
have expressed yours in no stinted measure."

" This country," he continued, " is to be the home

of a happy people. Surely you do not contemplate
a beast as you would a man."

" But why such reckless haste?" I replied, cooling
down a little.

" They are coming. Population everywhere seems
to be overcrowded. This land is being made ready
for them, and apparently none too soon. These creatures have lived here so long, and have kept the grass
so closely grazed, that the hot sun and dry winds
have made a desert of it. Perhaps the time was very
near when they could not have obtained food in the
winter, and then they would have perished with cold
and hunger. It will require a long time to redeem
the land and make it fit for cultivation. Maybe it
is all right. Who can tell?" Then, after reflecting
a moment, he asked: " When do you intend to resume your work ? "

"That is just what I want to talk about," I replied. " I would like to begin in the morning, and,
if agreeable to you, I will write while you dictate.
With both of us watching the points, I think very
little revision will be needed, and that we will be
able to push the work very rapidly; and, Flex, I
really think that some publisher will give us a good
sum for the copyright."

He made no reply, but looking up said : " The sky

is overcast with clouds; the night is near; we must make haste and ride fast or we will not be able to keep the course."

Then we mounted and rode rapidly home.

At breakfast the next morning, I noticed that the place usually occupied by my friend was vacant. Recollecting at the same time that my first important case stood for trial that day, I said:

"Tell Flex to be at the court room as soon as possible; I want him to hear my opening to the jury."

I won the case, but Flex came not that day nor the next; and weeks and months went by and still he came not.

Oh, how long the days seem when one hopes for something that never comes; the light of the office was gone; the gladsome laugh and cheery voice were gone, never to return again to that office. But I plodded on, working longer days and harder than ever. I never left the village; the country had lost its charms for me.

One rainy afternoon, something like a year after, while rummaging through neglected pigeon holes and drawers that contained nothing but old briefs and stale papers, I came across my old manuscript; it had rather a shabby appearance and time had browned it, but I gave it an affectionate look, thinking here is the key to the whole trouble, and I said to it, "To-morrow I will finish you out of hand."

The greater part of the next day I was busy in court. However, about four o'clock in the evening I pulled down the manuscript, and, glancing at the title-page, I said to myself in a congratulatory way : "You are right, my boy; that sounds as if the author had thoroughly studied his subject and knew all about it."

Dipping into the first chapter I began to grow nervous, and turning it quickly I looked again at the title-page.

"What stuff is this !" I exclaimed ; "Here is no originality, neither pith or point ; this is nothing but the thoughts of others remodelled, and a poor job at that." At the same time thrusting it into the stove, I savagely added, "now you are finished out of hand."

Then I resolved to write what I had learned of the reflex.

# CHAPTER II.

## WHAT IS MAGNETIC FORCE?

THE theory of the attraction of gravity has stood the test of every astronomical fact and mathematical calculation that has ever been applied to it. Nevertheless, it was demonstrated by Newton and others, that gravitation would only account for planetary motion already under way, and that the solar system would ultimately run down unless the effects of attraction were counteracted by some other positive force.

Indeed, astronomers and physicists in Newton's time, knew as well as we know, that no cosmology can be constructed with gravity alone as the motive power. And so one of them invented the phrase, "original impulse," and with it started the machinery. Then, still finding a scientific vacancy, he added centrifugal force to his invention and endeavored to show that nature had so constructed a perpetual motion.

This theory has been accepted regardless of the fact that original impulse is not a scientific thing in any sense, and that centrifugal force is no force at all but inertia.

How often have we been shown that a planetary body propelled by original impulse in a right line would soon be deflected by gravitation and forced to move in a circular or an elliptical orbit.

No one ever doubted it the first time it was explained to him, and no one has ever doubted it since. But why were the planets started moving in right lines? Could not original impulse as easily propelled them somewhat in the direction they were intended to pursue?

Supposing the theory to be true; what would have been the condition of the universe when all the heavenly bodies began to change their courses and take up new and entirely different ones?

Of course, it was an illustration, but it was intended to illustrate gravity as an universal motive power. And, unfortunately for science, or at least for the theory, it proved too much, for it will be conceded that an attractive force sufficient to deflect the course of a planet moving in a right line, would settle the career of that planet shortly thereafter.

It has been but a few years since we began to consider light, heat, magnetism, galvanism, electricity, etc., as natural forces. In the school books of the

early part of this century, they were denominated the
"imponderable substances." And it was explained
that heat, which it was thought could be better understood by calling it caloric, expanded the metals, rari-
fied the gases and decomposed all organic substances.

At the beginning of the last century, light was
thought to be composed of corpuscles ; and the sun
was supposed to contain a never-failing supply of
them. By what means they were shot across the
chasm from the sun to us, was a great puzzle, with
which Newton, Bentley, and a host of German,
French and English philosophers wrestled during
the greater part of their lives.

Now the corpuscles are gone ; but the puzzle remains with us, and is not likely to be solved until we
fully recognize that resisted force is heat ; and that
when force is impeded by the atmosphere it is light.

The first conclusion is not new by any means ;
neither may the second be, but one is led to think
that both are, when noticing how little attention is
paid to them by philosophers who speculate on the
subject of solar light and heat.

It was the undulatory theory of light that settled
the career of the little corpuscles.

To undulate, means to move backward and forward, to vibrate. What is it, then, that is vibrating

and is light? Is it the particles of the air or is it the particles of an universal ether?

Shall we say it is the ether, and enter the domain of wild conjecture where no one can follow? Shall we now discuss the properties of material about which nobody knows anything and so avoid all criticism? Or shall we say it is the air and take the consequences of an erroneous conclusion?

After the brilliant corpuscles had about faded from the memory of men, came the vibratory theory of heat. This theory is founded on the assumption that heat or rather temperature is a sensation derived from a movement of the ultimate particles or atoms of matter. The idea is, that when these atoms are in moderate temperature, their movement is so slight that we are unable to recognize it except by the sense of feeling; that as the temperature increases the movement becomes greater, and exceedingly more rapid, so that we recognize it in the incandescence of the body and the light produced by the force operating in its particles; that still greater temperature causes the dissolution of organic substances by the forceful separation of their parts. No reasonable objection has ever been made to this theory.

Sir Humphry Davy says, "Heat, then, or that power which prevents the actual contact of bodies, and which is the cause of our peculiar sensations of heat and cold, may be defined a peculiar motion, probably a vibration of the corpuscles of bodies tending to separate them."

In his chemical philosophy published in 1812, he says:

"The immediate cause of the phenomenon is motion."

. Now, as motion can only be conceived as the effect of force previously or presently applied, it follows that light and darkness, high and low temperature require some scientific primary force to produce them. What is this force?

If light and high temperature are the effects of rapid motion, and darkness and cold of slower motion, is it not probable that the condition of absolute darkness and entire absence of heat (temperature) does not exist anywhere in the universe? But that where there is the least matter, that is to say, where matter only exists in its most tenuous conditions; there will be also the nearest approximation to absolute darkness and cold.

This being admitted, leads to the almost certain conclusion that as we rise from the earth into space it is not only the temperature that is decreasing, but also the light is diminishing in the same ratio; that while no place can be found or imagined where either light or heat are absolutely absent, yet a place would soon be reached when both would be comparatively absent; and we may also conclude that when such place is reached it will be found comparatively a vacuum.

During the time these theories of force and its phenomena were being advanced and brought to our knowledge, investigation and experiment were being pushed all along the line. And electricity and a class of phenomena apparently more nearly allied to it began to occupy the public mind. And now we have the electric light, and heat, and power derived from the currents of primary force.

Generally it may be said that the manifestations of a thing are not the thing itself. Yet, as to primary force, we can at present form no conception of it except such as we derive from its phenomena; and as these have all been given separate names, it becomes necessary that primary force itself should have a name, for without it there can be no certainty of expression when discussing problems in which forceful phenomena are involved.

New names are objectionable; they should never be given to an old subject, they are apt to distract the mind at a time when clearness of perception is

indispensable. For obvious reasons the choice of old
names lies between electricity and magnetism.

Electric force is new to us; its power has been discovered or rather brought into use as it were yesterday, and to-day we make a servant of it to carry
messages, light our homes and to transport ourselves
and our burdens. These improvements, following
each other in quick succession, have created a literature in which electricity is the central figure. Consequently the word has acquired a restricted meaning.
Indeed, it has been so intimately connected with a
particular class of phenomena that it is now nearly if
not quite impossible to use it as a name for the force
involved in world-formation.

Magnetism is the older name; as a mere question
of taste it is preferable. Like all old names it has a
certain dignity of sound not found in the word electricity. Magnetism has always been the most occult
force in nature; apparently it yields no signs except
those of the simplest and most impressive character.
It is a lode-stone that ever silently points; in the full
grandeur of its power it will not be a servant. Let
us, then, for the time being, accept the name and apply
it to the scientific force underlying all natural phenomena.

Magnetic force is not derived from gravitation;

nor from the decomposition of organic substances; nor from the expansion or contraction of matter within earthly limits. It is more nearly the cause of these things than the effect of them. Considered as a primary force, we have all the knowledge of it we can have of anything; we feel it, see it, taste it and smell it every day of our lives. It is the fragrance of the rose and the stench of the cesspool.

Such a subject cannot be examined by one generation of men and explained by the next. It reaches backward to the time when God said: " Let there be light! " and forward into eternity. The theory of its operation may not be demonstrated during the life period of a race of men.

Since this is the case, whatever hypothesis conforms to, and explains the greatest number of phenomena and appears antagonistic to the least number will be accepted. This is the crucial test; it is not at present a question of absolute truth, but a question of the nearest approximation thereto.

Then what is magnetic force? Where does it come from? Where does it go?

Having so stated the subjects I intended to treat I began to feel a nervous chill passing through my body and a cold perspiration gathering on my brow.

What is magnetic force? I repeated; can it be

possible that I have forgotten these things? I must
be laboring under some mistake. Have I actually
lost the keys or did I ever have them? Beginning
to feel desperate I rose and walked the floor; this
partially quieted my excitement, and I sat down
again and read the manuscript until I again reached
the unanswerable questions. *What is magnetic force?*
*Where does it come from? Where does it go?*

There was no answer, and I thought I would give
the price of the best tract of land in the county for
just five minutes talk with Flex, but there was no
hope of that.

Then feeling bitter toward the world and all there
is in it, I rolled up the manuscript and placed it in a
pigeon hole saying to myself:

"What is there in this world but work and dollars?
I will resume my profession; hereafter I will hew to
no line but the legal line. *This is the law* shall be
my motto, and whatsoever it gives to me or to any
man, that shall he have and no more."

After that my office looked like a den; it was a den,
and the years passed on.

In the year 1883, my wife's health became broken
and being advised by our physician she went to
the sea-side, taking our youngest son with her for
company. The oldest and only other child had

already entered life for himself, and so I was left
alone.

Oh, how lonesome a house seems which was once
a home, but is now only a furnished building. The
master remains but its light and hope and cheerful-
ness have fled. Have you ever noticed at such a
time how the continual click-clack of the clock re-
sounds through every room ? How strange it is that
a cheerful old family clock should have become a
misanthrope, and persist in repeating the word, never,
never, never, never, as if it intended to emphasize the
fact that Christ will never again stand at your door
and knock. At such a time one is apt to take a re-
trospect of one's life, and the manner in which it has
been spent ; at least I did ; and among other unpleasant things there came to my mind, the old work that
I had destroyed ; the visit and departure of the reflex ; the new manuscript then more than six years
old ; and I thought, perhaps, I have been too easily
discouraged. Maybe if I had persevered, I might
have overcome all the difficulties. To-morrow, I will
read that manuscript and thoroughly reflect upon it.

The next year the doctor advised a permanent
change of climate, and we broke up our home and
started to travel. During the five years thereafter,
we visited many of the natural wonders in our own

country, and some in foreign lands, and then we established our residence in Washington.

For a few months, I took pleasure in examining the public buildings; the collection of models in the patent office, the Smithsonian Institute, the Corcoran Art Gallery, and then I settled down as a regular visitor at the Capitol.

Here was a building erected regardless of cost; adorned with frescoes that had taken half a lifetime to execute; here were statues that great states had deemed worthy to present to the nation. Here, also one might hear the speech of a statesman, or listen to the harangue of a demagogue. On the whole it was just the place for me to spend a quiet hour or two with my own thoughts and speculations.

How long I continued to enjoy this I cannot say, but after while I became weary, and then I began to think of my past experience.

One afternoon I was sitting at home with my feet against the side of the fire-place in the old law-office style; I had been thinking of old times; it seemed to me that all had gone well, that our troublous days had been very few. Indeed, it seemed as if they had all been bright and happy ones, and I longed to have them over again. I thought what a pleasure it would be to circle with friends around a camp-fire and eat buffalo meat. I felt sure that no meat in Washington was half as good; and so I said to the brave little wife who had been with us in all the Kansas calamities, "I have made up my mind to visit Oklahoma next week."

"I hope you will not think of such a thing," she replied; "I would remain here this winter and enjoy the comforts of the city and its entertainments. The territory is a wild country; its comforts are few, its hardships many."

"I want to see the plains," I said, "and hear the crack of a rifle and the rough voices of frontiersmen."

"You cannot turn the hands on life's clock backward," she very gently replied. And then reflecting a moment, added: "Since time drags so heavily, why do you not finish your treatise."

"That is just what I will do," I said, rising and going toward ——. And then I resumed my seat, thinking, what is the use. Don't I know the situation of affairs in that manuscript? *What is magnetic force?*

It was a bitter recollection, and I fiercely put on my great coat and strode to the Capitol.

Seated in the rotunda, I soon began to take an interest in the crowd of sight-seers. They are from all

parts of the country; their manner and dress quite
different, but usually in good form; the seats are
tolerably well filled; here and there small groups of
men stand chatting and smoking cigars. Two young
men in sailor's garb are looking at the picture of De
Soto discovering the Mississippi river; three or four
sisters of charity have just gone out at the east door.
My thoughts are on none of these things; there are
several ladies, evidently from abroad. The guides
are describing the paintings and other things in a
low voice, that comes to me in fragments: "That
Bronze Door;" "Fifty-six Thousand Dollars;"
"The Baptism of Pocahontas;" "Seven Years;"
"The Surrender of Lord Cornwallis." All this was
lost to me. My thoughts had drifted along with a
small company into the old house of representatives,
now an art gallery. I saw the mosaic of Abraham
Lincoln, and thought about his life and services and
the prominent place occupied by him in later American history. Turning a little to the left, there stood
the colossal statue of Ethan Allen; contributed by
the State of Vermont, done by L. C. Mead; and I
thought, here is a sculptor who conceived the image
and the spirit of a military hero, and summoned him
from the times of Bunker Hill and Quebec. Out of
cold marble he has created it, and placed it here

in his country's capitol ; I was filled with emotion ;
and I said, "Heavenly Father! All these years I
have faithfully studied the works of thy creation,
hoping to find enlightenment that would enable me
to finish my work. Thou only knowest how hard I
have tried to wring the secret out of nature itself, and
that I have found thy flaming sword guarding it at
every point; now all has failed and I come to thee."

At this time a small company were passing toward
the senate chamber, and a familiar form parted from
them and approaching me rapidly said, "Do you remember me?"

"Indeed, I do, you are my old Kansas friend."

"I am the reflex."

"Yes, I know, but why did you not return?"

"I was not permitted," he replied, and then placing his arm in mine he said : "Will you go with
me?"

"Anywhere," I answered, and we walked together
as we had years before.

"How are you getting on with your work?" he
asked.

Then I related what I had done with the old work,
the commencement of the new one, and I was about
to recount the places I had visited, when he interrupted me and said :

"You may forbear, I was with you; I have been with you on every mountain top and in every valley, I have laid beside you on the hot sands of the Yellowstone, while sulphurous steam and ominous growlings issued from every fissure. There we saw the great geyser's outburst and heard the roar of the hot water as it fell to the earth and ran in scalding streams to the river. I knew your thoughts all the time, but I had no message; now I am sent to refresh your memory. And I have brought you to this place so that you may realize the importance of the message, and receive it in the presence of your country's capitol."

And he handed me a folded manuscript. As I received it I saw that we were standing on the dome of the capitol.

"Dear friend," I said, "Will you not remain and help me revise what I have written? it is so very imperfect."

"I cannot," he replied, "I am strictly enjoined not to interfere with your work at this time." "Then," said I, "since you have failed me I will put my trust in the Lord God Omnipotent."

"And then you may rely on the reflex," he replied.

He was gone;—the twinkling stars were shining brightly in the heavens. Beneath; the great arc-lights of the city blazed and scintillated, and I thought shall I ever know ;— *What is magnetic force? Where does it come from? Where does it go?* Then a cold wind swept across the summit of the building, and with it came from afar off the sonorous voice of a minister reading to his people.

"Seek ye first the kingdom of God and His righteousness, and all these things shall be added unto you."

Then I drew my coat more closely about me and descended the stairs.

The manuscript was superscribed at my old home in Kansas, dated November 6, 1876, and addressed to me personally.

I will read :

"These pages are written with a three-fold object; the first is to view the force we call magnetism at its fountain-head, and learn by analogy from whence it came, and what may have been among the first works thereof.

"In the second place, will be presented such phenomena as tend more or less directly to prove the main theory, and particularly such as remain unexplained on other hypotheses.

"The third object, you are supposed to be in frame of mind to contemplate without special explanation

at this time.  If you are not you may as well abandon the subject at once;  for you are admonished
that you never will realize the glory of the heavenly
bodies, nor understand their condition and the relation they bear to each other, until you have cast off all
the grosser abstractions derived from your present
environment.

"You must know that in the universe distance is
a secondary consideration.  Miles have no relation to
infinite space.  Time is but the measure of passing
events.  Unfortunately, there are grosser conceptions
which will occur to you; these are a murderous weight.
There lies the ' valley and the shadow of death.'  It
may not be amiss to call your attention to an every-
day example of this.

" In the suburbs of the city there is an electro-dynamo; a single wire forms a circuit; to the small boys
it seems a very simple contrivance and apparently of
no use at all.  Many men talk of its usefulness, and
there is no end of preaching its merits and proclaiming the danger of improperly using it.

"A very small boy says, ' I know all this talk
about it is nonsense, I believe it is confined to weak-
minded people; I intend to pay no attention to it.'
He talks in this way, thinks in this way, until the
admonition of his elders has left his mind; he has

lost all fear of the wire; audaciously he takes hold of it with both hands; he is dead!

"In the field we are about to enter, condition is everything; things are near or far from each other with reference to their condition. This is an axiom in a higher science than we are now considering.

"If you disregard the admonition here given, you will not be able to understand the thesis nor follow its sequences to their ultimate conclusion; you will forget yourself; the full dignity of a man will depart from you, and the mighty events of an eternity past will sweep on through an endless future without your having any knowledge of them. Had there been no laws in force except such as you have heretofore deemed scientific, this would have been your condition; you had became so engrossed with affairs which were of little consequence to you, that you forgot the Great First Cause.

"You boldly attempted to construct an universal theory with the Creator of it all left out; and you are not to forget that you failed.

"You are again reminded that magnetic force is an expression of the conflicting relationship subsisting between the bodies of matter that compose the universe. Not only between the heavenly bodies, but between every particle of matter in the universe, whether the same be gaseous, aqueous, or solid.

"The first expression of this force operates in the line of unlike presentation ; it is, therefore, an attractive force in polar direction, causing the aggregation of diffused matter into worlds. This is an universal condition.

" Its second expression is that of repulsion where the like poles of two magnetic bodies of matter are presented to each other. This is also an universal condition.

" Its third expression is the equilibrial effect of attraction and repulsion. It is, therefore, an expanding and contracting force.

" These counter-forces cause the whole universe to tremble, and every particle of matter to be in a continual state of vibration. For this reason, matter assumes the three forms referred to, air, earth and water. Correctly speaking, magnetic force cannot be said to be moving in any direction. But it causes material to move, and therefore a knowledge of its operations can be more easily acquired by considering that it exists in currents. After while, you will be able to comprehend it as a rectilineal contraction toward an infinite number of centres in certain directions. A rectilineal expansion from the same centres in other

directions, and a curvilinear adjustment acting intermediately between them in all directions. But this
is a profound thesis. You will not be able to thoroughly understand it until you abandon the idea that
north and south, east and west, right and left, up and
down are universal terms.

"*What is magnetic force?*" It is the expansion and
contraction of the universe consequent to the fact,
that each particle of matter in it is striving to
maintain its individuality. Where does it come
from ? It is the power of God, and therefore an
ever-present reality. You may consider it the dividing line from which the heavenly sciences ascend
and those of earth descend. Make its three expressions your study, and all the natural phenomena
will marshal themselves in their proper order.

"*You will write !*"

# CHAPTER III.

## WORLD FORMATION.

ASTRONOMERS who have studied the structure of the solar system, are of the opinion that it was once a nebula. And that the changes which have taken place have been accomplished by the natural forces inherent in matter.

More than two centuries ago, René Descartes conceived the idea that universal space was at first filled with particles of ether or fluid matter endowed with a rapid spiral motion ; with these vortices he endeavored to explain the formation of the universe and the movements of the heavenly bodies.

"The general idea now entertained is that primordial matter has accomplished the work of world formation by the action of gravity aided by molecular forces. It is assumed by some, that on physical principles, primordial matter widely distributed would pass through the following changes : Gravitation would cause the mass to contract and become more dense ; this would be followed by atomic repulsion which, acting against gravitation, would produce heat. After a certain degree of condensation had taken place, molecular combination would result. This would be followed by radiation and precipitation of the binary atoms as floculi floating in the rarer medium. These floculi will tend toward a common centre, but as the mass is irregular the motion will be really to one side of the centre. This will result in a spiral movement. Mutual attraction will produce groups of floculi moving around local centres of gravity. There will be here and there detached portions, which will not coalesce with the larger internal masses, but will slowly follow, thus accounting for the formation of comets."—*Library of Universal Knowledge*, vol. x., p. 450.*

Continued investigation and discovery furnishes strong indications pointing to the conclusion that the natural phenomena, light, temperature, magnetism, electricity, etc., all spring from one primary force, and that the simplest manifestation of this force may be found in a common magnet. Faraday says:

"I have long held an opinion amounting almost to a conviction, in common, I believe, with many other lovers of natural knowledge, that the various forms under which the forces of matter are made manifest, have one common origin."

It may be considered as an established fact, that the earth is a magnet, and that there is a magnetic connection between it and the sun. It needs then

---

* An admirable presentation of the nebular hypothesis written by the late Richard A. Proctor, may be found in the *American Cyclopædia*, vol. xi., p. 201.

only to be stated, that the sun and the planets are magnets; and if so, why not the asteroids and comets, and, indeed, every particle of matter existing anywhere in the interstellar spaces? This seems to be the legitimate conclusion.

Then may we not assume that the solar nebula was composed of material, every particle of which was endowed, in like manner as the earth is endowed, with the power of attraction and repulsion and consequent polarity and axial direction.*

There is no doubt that the solar nebula contained all the elemental ingredients found in the earth, and that its particles were capable of exhibiting in a feeble manner the phenomena of temperature, light, and perhaps others.

We say in a feeble manner, for it is certain that the magnetic strength increases as the size of the aggregations increased. And this being true as to magnetism, it is doubtless true as to temperature and other phenomena. From this we infer that the temperature of the nebula and its particles was very low at first, and that as aggregation proceeded it increased

---

* Repellant power is not usually ascribed to the earth; but to deny it is to deny that it is a magnet. If it be a magnet, it surely would repel another planet if a "like presentation" of them occurred.

and the heat tended towards the centre of the aggregations ; and we assume that this process is still under
way.

The polarity of the needle depends on its being a
magnet; its axial direction depends on the fact that
the earth is a magnet. In like manner, we may say
the polarity of the earth depends on its being a magnet,
but on what does its axial direction depend? Herschel says :

"In the annual motion of the earth, its axis preserves at
all times the same direction as if the orbital movement had
no existence ; and is carried round parallel to itself and pointing always to the same vanishing point in the sphere of the
fixed stars."*—*Outlines of Astronomy*, sec. 362.

We are taught that the solar system is only a small
portion of an infinite universe ; and that the force of
gravity is universal. I am prepared to accept both
conclusions because I believe the force of gravity to
be simply an expression of magnetic attraction, and
that its complement, the force of repulsion, is also
universal. I would enlarge the idea conveyed by the
word gravitation, so as to bring the force meant by

---

* The earth undergoes considerable changes of axial direction during the precessional period, but this fact does not
weaken the force of any conclusions drawn from its axial stability.

it into correlation with the magnetic phenomena; and then, I conceive, that polarity and axial direction will take their proper places in the economy of the solar system.

We are unable to fully understand what force is, even under local circumstances. How much more, when the processes we ascribe to it begin to assume infinite proportions. Nevertheless, I venture to offer the following hypotheses.

I suggest that magnetic force exists in three circuits,* and that axial direction is the effect of the currents of the first circuit, acting north and south through our system and other systems in the same circuit, and generally connecting our system and each member thereof, whether the same be the sun, a planet, an atom, or a molecule, with the entire universe of matter, thereby causing their polar magnetic relation to be the same as that which would exist between magnetic beads strung in a circle, Fig. 1.

Choosing the north simply for a starting point and the earth for an example, the first circuit approaches the earth in a curved line from the next system lying north of ours; reaching the north pole it merges in the earth's second and third circuits, after which it

---

* The word circuits is used as a convenient term. I mean by it simply universal forceful expressions.

proceeds from the south pole in a curved line to the
next system lying south of ours, and from thence

Fig. 1.

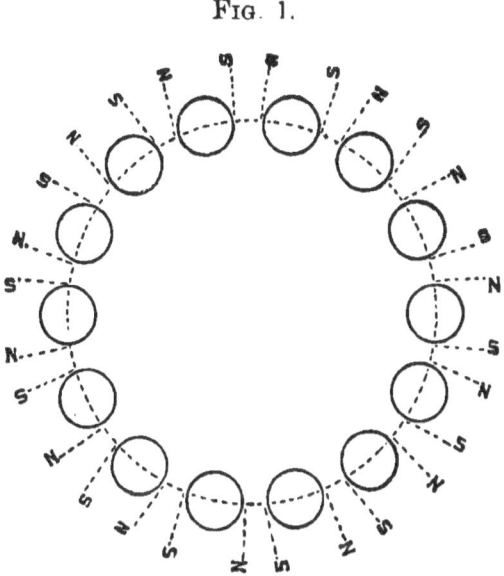

through all the systems in the same circuit, forming
an ellipse or circle to the place of beginning.*

It will be seen that this circuit is universal in
every sense. Owing to its position in polar directions all the particles of matter within its course are
arranged as shown in Fig. 1, with their unlike poles

---

* These descriptions are made to conform to the popular
idea of magnetic currents. Personally, I conceive magnetic
force to be more in the nature of a stretched rubber cord, in
which slight and infinitely rapid changes of tension are constantly taking place.

presented to, and in fact impinging on each other. Therefore it is an attractive aggregative circuit.

The currents of the second circuit enter the earth at its north magnetic parallel.* From thence they proceed toward the centre of the earth to the heated margin,† thence following the dips and sinuosities of the heated margin to a corresponding radius at the south magnetic parallel ; thence emerging at the place last mentioned they return on the outside of the earth to the place of beginning. Fig. 2 shows a single line of both circuits.

The return of the second circuit through the at-

---

* The north is again simply taken as a starting point. The magnetic parallels do not conform to any geographical degree of latitude. Certain points of magnetic intensity have been called the "true magnetic poles ;" these are sometimes found north and sometimes south of what may be called the mean magnetic parallel.

† When a magnet is heated to redness it loses permanently every trace of magnetism. Iron also at a red heat ceases to be attracted by the magnet. At temperatures below red heat the magnet parts with some of its power, the loss increasing with the temperature. The temperature at which other substances affected by the magnet lose their magnetism, differs from that of iron. Cobalt remains magnetic at the highest temperature, and nickel loses this property at 662° Fahrenheit.—*Universal Library*, vol. ix., p. 362.

mosphere is somewhat in the tortuous direction of its inward route.

Fig. 2.

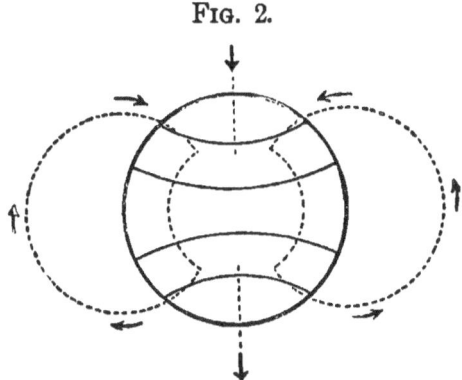

From which it appears that the circuits form a junctional union at the magnetic poles; and that within the body of the earth they are separated by the heated portions of the earth. Of course the absence of one form of force means the presence of another. That is the third circuit.

Fig. 3.

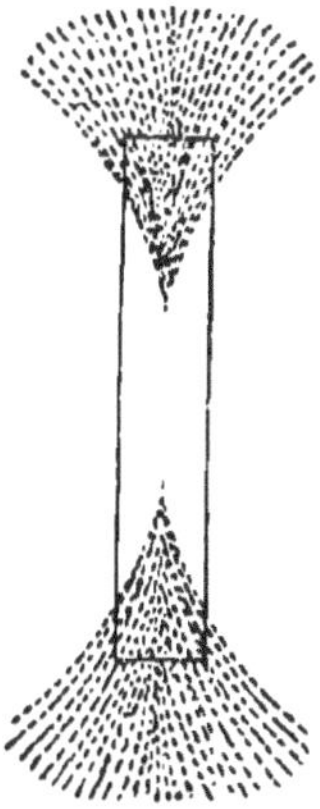

If we dip a magnet in iron-filings, they will adhere to it as in Fig. 3.

Lay a sheet of paper on a magnet and sprinkle iron-filings upon it, they will arrange themselves as in Fig. 4.

The first example shows attraction, and therefore, the course of the first circuit. That the magnet possesses any other force does not appear; because the filings having been repelled from the centre of it

FIG. 4.

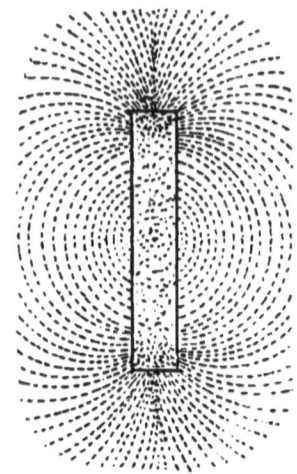

their weight has carried them away.

The second example shows both attraction and repulsion; but as the repellant force is not sufficient to overcome both weight and friction, and push the filings out to their proper places, the course of the second circuit is not perfectly exhibited.

We assume, that if the magnet and filings could be freely suspended, the latter would be found arranged as in Fig. 5.

FIG. 5.

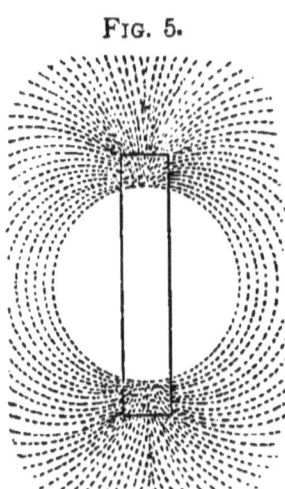

So far we have had only an equatorial view of a magnet and its forces in plane. Fig. 6, represents a polar projection of the same magnet. Here repulsion, or the third circuit, is all that appears.

Pictures can go no further.

If we desire to see a magnet with all its forces in operation at once, we must imagine it and the filings

in perfect suspension : absolutely *in equilibrio.* Then
we can see the extremities of the magnet gathering
in and incorporating the filings,
and its central parts at the same
time pushing them off. And
we can also see that though
the magnet is a bar, the material and the operation assume
at once a spherical shape.

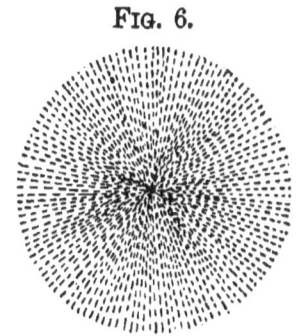

FIG. 6.

Now leaving this example,
and assuming that Fig. 4 is the earth, and studying
its forces in plane, we find that as the joint forces of
the first and second circuits are examined northward
from the north magnetic parallel to the north pole,
they represent more and more the influence of the
system lying north; until at the pole itself, the
filings on the magnet and the magnetic needle on
the earth stand vertical; showing that the sun has
lost its power, and that the system lying north has
assumed full control.

We also find, that as the force of the second circuit is examined southward from the north magnetic
pole to the equator, it gradually becomes more and
more repellant until at the magnetic equator* it is

* The magnetic equator does not conform to the geographical equator.

fully so. And there are no filings attached to the magnet and the needle lies horizontal on the earth, proving that such change has taken place.

From the junctional union we have endeavored to describe, springs the third circuit. It is the true physical expression of the counter-forces involved, that is to say, the dynamical effect of two forces acting in different directions.

The currents of the third circuit are supposed to flow around the earth from east to west. Therefore, its course is at right angles to that of the solar and earthly first circuits; at acute angles to their second circuits, and exactly in the opposite direction to the course of the sun's third circuit, which we assume also flows from east to west.

The existence of the first circuit is shown by the polarity and axial direction of the earth, sun and planets. The existence of the second is proven by the inclination and declination of the magnetic needle.

The third circuit is more occult. It is, indeed, one of nature's profound secrets. So much so that it required the magical skill of one of the most eminent physicists of modern times to discover it.*

Considered from one aspect, the second and third

---

* André Marie Ampere.

circuits seem to be local ; from another, universal. It
is probable that all or nearly all the electrical phenomena under our control spring from these two circuits. The tension of the first circuit may be so
great that its forces cannot be drawn from except by
the processes of chemical union or dissolution.

It has been briefly stated that the earth's third circuit flows in an exactly opposite direction to the
course of the same circuit of the sun, and yet that
both flow from east to west. For example, draw two
circles opposite to each other on thin paper, Fig. 7.
Indicate the direction of the currents from east to
west, that is, from right to left, as maps are con-

FIG. 7.

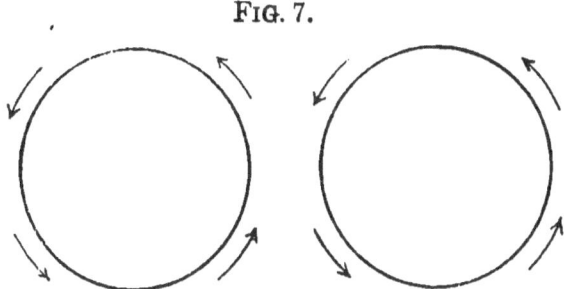

structed. You will observe that though both currents are apparently running from east to west, yet
where they approach each other they are running in
opposite directions.

Now place the paper between yourself and a strong
light. Look at the figure through the paper. You

discover that the direction of the currents has apparently changed by merely changing the point of observation, so that they now appear to be running from west to east. One thing remains unchanged. They are still running in opposite directions.

We learn from this figure that east and west, right and left, may be misleading terms when they are applied to a rotary movement.

Let us linger with this figure just a moment and imagine that it is a mechanical contrivance; that the circles are iron cog-wheels rapidly rotating. Now bring them together as if you would place them in gear. You realize that they will not follow each other in train, but that they will rebound and that the sparks will fly. In fact they will repel each other because they *are* running in different directions.

However, the figure is not intended to illustrate a mere mechanical movement, but to explain the currents of the third circuits around the earth and sun; each flowing from east to west and yet in opposite directions, and so offering a reason for the magnetic law that " *Currents running in the same direction attract and those in opposite directions repel.*"

When the reason for a law is known the law itself is not very soon forgotten.

It follows from the premises that the earth and sun

repel each other because of the "like presentation" of their poles, and that their third circuits are expressions of the fact.

As to the production of light and heat, we will offer the following suggestions :

If the analogies heretofore considered be sufficient to warrant the conclusion that every particle of matter in interstellar space is a magnet, then the molecules or atoms of our atmosphere are magnets, and in such case the currents under consideration are as numerous as the molecules, and the latter are arranged in the form indicated by the magnetic needle, that is to say, lying horizontal at the equator and standing perpendicular at the magnetic parallels and at the poles. From which it arises, that as the diurnal revolution of the earth proceeds, the currents of the solar second circuit are forced through the earth's atmospheric molecules lengthwise at the equator, and angularly at the magnetic parallels, and the molecules being already charged, are in this way subjected to an overcharge which renders them transparent and causes them to glow with magnetic excitement, *i.e.*, force. This overcharge we infer is light.

To be more explicit. As diurnal revolution proceeds there are rapid changes of magnetic presentation taking place, caused by the attractive currents crossing the repellant currents in the molecules of the air. These changes of presentation are similar to those that take place in an electro-dynamo.

The tenuous atmosphere farther away from the earth and the sun being under so much greater tension, its molecules are in condition to receive and transmit the mutual force of the two bodies without exhibiting any phenomena except the lowest,—darkness and cold.

The overcharge proceeds toward the earth; reaching the ground-line its direction is changed by the full force of the earth's currents and it then proceeds toward the nearest magnetic pole. This change of direction causes increased vibration in the particles of solid matter, and this is heat.

The intensity of solar heat depends entirely on the sharpness of the angle made by the advancing currents after reaching the earth or some of its constituents.

In this way we may account for the intense heat of the sun when its rays are vertical, and its diminution when the angle of incidence is less. Herein is also the reason why the air will not readily receive heat from the sun but will from the earth. The overcharge from the sun is not heat but force, which only becomes heat when it is resisted.

We will now commence at a time when our solar system and those adjacent to it, north and south, formed a continuous body of primordial matter.*

Assuming its particles to be arranged as shown in Fig. 1, they would then be undergoing magnetic combination, chemical union and condensation. This process would be likely to create central aggregations, and nebular segregation would then be the inevitable result, that is to say, the nebulous matter surrounding certain centres would be drawn away from that surrounding other centres by the shrinkage resulting from interior condensation at the different stations in the first circuit.

After separation, the particles composing our solar nebula would still be undergoing the same process, and as attraction in our nebula would be acting against the same force in those lying north and south of it, condensation would take place more rapidly at its centre and accordingly there we find the greatest aggregation. For the same reason, while aggregations might take place anywhere in the nebula, the most important of them would be located near its equatorial plane.

---

* We assume primordial matter to be aqueous vapor containing all the elemental ingredients and that the air is a clarified sample of it.

In these situations no doubt solid matter was first developed.

Accordingly the sun and all the planets acquired a solid nucleus comparatively near the same time. Their growth has been the effect of precisely the same processes, therefore a description of the growth of one of them will be in a general way a description of all the others.

Now let the sun be an example. Conceive it as a small spherical body located in the centre of the nebula, the latter extending far beyond the present limits of the system. Bear in mind that it is enveloped with particles of matter, each endowed with polarity and axial direction. Such being the case, is it not more than probable that it has aggregated in the past, and still is aggregating similar to the manner in which iron-filings attach themselves to a bar magnet? With this difference : that in the example of a magnet the process is instantly begun and finished, while in the case of the sun it is continuous and possibly endless, on account of the outside resistance referred to.

We may then say that the flow of primordial matter began at both poles of the sun, forming at first right line extensions to its axis and moving toward its centre. As the material sank into the sun

the central tension became greater and greater and
the flow spread out in the form of a funnel, moving
farther and farther away from the rectilinear, leaving
the spaces passed over still occupied by the rarer
medium (Fig. 8).*    The effect of this was threefold.

First.—The flow became vortical; this form of
motion being superinduced by the angularity of the

FIG. 8.

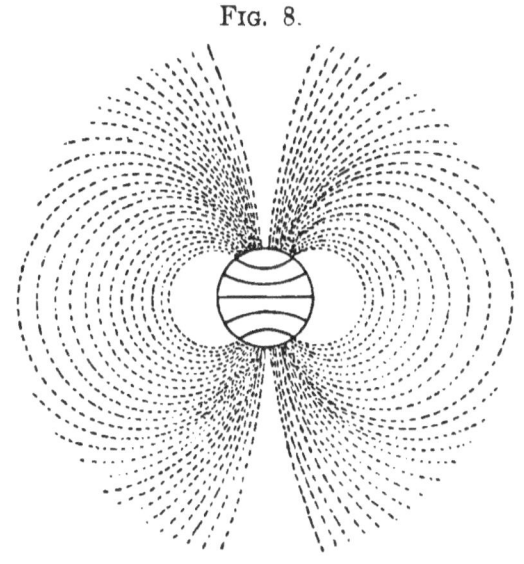

movement acting against the stability of the axial
direction of the sun and the incoming bodies.

Second.—The attraction between the sun and the

---

* Fig. 8 is intended to show only that portion of the nebula
in the immediate neighborhood of the sun. The nebula is
to be imagined as extending outwardly and as having other
aggregations taking place in it.

bodies composing the flow became more and more tangential as the size of the bodies increased ; causing the sun to rotate and also a similar but more rapid rotation of the other bodies involved.

Third.—The perfectly attractive presentation that existed at the beginning of the flow became more and more indirect as the angle of arrival and departure increased. Ultimately the flow reached an angle suf-

FIG. 9.

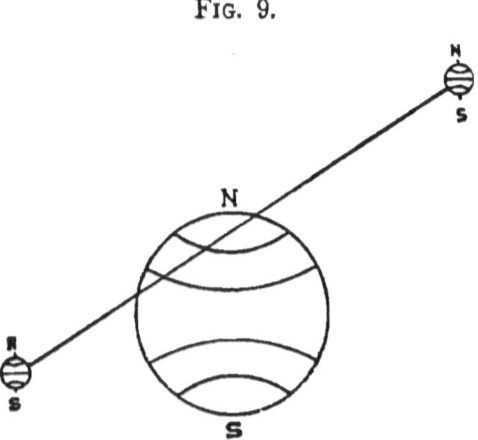

ficient to change the presentation from *unlike* to *like;* and then the incoming bodies were repelled. But before this took place, there was a field passed over from which the bodies presented their like poles to the sun at their nearest approach, and being repelled they made a complete vortical orbital revolution ; still attracted at their aphelion, but repelled at their perihelion passages, Fig. 9.

These are the comets; they may be considered rudimentary planets. They are as nearly a well bal-
anced planet as the polar flow can produce.

As to their orbits, we remark that elliptical orbits
are the exponent of the unequal forces acting on the
bodies moving in them; therefore, they become more

FIG. 10.

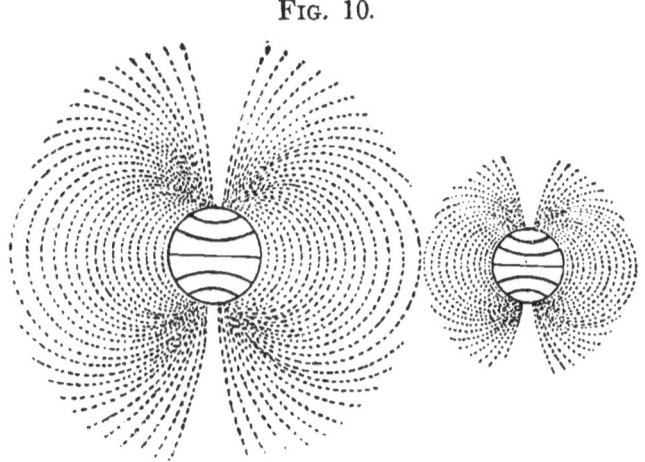

circular from time to time, that being the equilibrial
form of curvilineal motion. If the ellipse is greatly
elongated the change of course takes place more
rapidly.

Now let the earth be an example; imagine that it
has contemporaneously undergone the same processes
until its polar vortices have reached those of the sun.
The attractive forces of the solar and earthly first circuits are now contending for the same material in the
same field. This is not an example of bar-magnets.

The tremendous energies of two heavenly bodies have met in the amphitheatre of the solar system; the result is certain. The earth's comets, if there be any, are swept away in an instant to whirl in a vortex; the earth itself would follow. It did follow, but being firmly held by the same force at both poles it started steadily on its first orbital revolution, Fig. 10.

The earth then having been given its rotary and its orbital movement by attractive force, will a mere tendency to "fly off at a tangent," if it had such a tendency, prevent it from reaching the sun? Is there any probability that it would be a great length of time getting there? Would it not fly swiftly in constantly diminishing circles or ellipses to its destination? Philosophers answer these questions by suggesting that "*the machinery of the heavens is running down.*"

Attraction cannot be conceived as anything but an aggregative force; it must be met by some positive counter-force which is either equal to it, or at least able to contend with it forever. Without such a preservative force, the solar system is unbalanced; nay more, the universe is unbalanced, and cannot be conceived as an endless reality.

The course of the earth's second circuit has been described. It enters the earth at one of its magnetic poles and emerges at the other. If you look again at the magnet, Fig. 5, you will see that it is apparently attractive at the places mentioned. Now when the polar flow of the earth and sun reached their respective magnetic poles, it encountered the force of their respective second circuits acting at angles to it; and repulsion was the immediate result. This prevented the flow from proceeding farther toward the centre of either of the bodies. For then the physical fact that the north pole of the earth is at all times indirectly presented to the north pole of the sun, and its south pole to the south pole of the sun, began to have force and effect. And they repelled each other at every point in the earth's orbit.

Therefore the earth may be considered as being carried around the sun by its first circuit of attractive force and firmly pressed all the way around against the mutual repellant forces of the solar and earthly second circuits. And since the forces are not equal to each other in this example, the earth pursues an elliptical orbit.

It is possible that the earth's orbit was at first more elongated than it is at present. Its aphelion distance may have been greater and its perihelion less. There are indications pointing to the conclusion that it once circulated more nearly about the southern poles of the sun. This may be the reason that the arctic regions of the earth are so much better stocked with fauna and flora than its antarctic regions. But reflections of this kind are not within the scope of our hypothesis.

Our satellite, the moon, is only 240,000 miles from the earth; a magnetic connection between it and the earth must have taken place at a very early period, perhaps thousands of years before the earth fell under the influence of the sun. Such a connection may have been the occasion of more important results than we are inclined to imagine. We are impressed with this idea when we reflect that both bodies may have been— indeed, must have been—surrounded with a denser atmosphere, and hence a deeper one than now. And that they then formed a comparatively independent system; the earth at that time may have had comets circulating about its northern and southern poles. And the moon may have shone with a brilliancy not to be conceived at present.* However this may be, three great circuits of magnetic force were undoubtedly established when the earth and moon entered into binary relationship.

---

* If the moon ever had any comets they probably fell to the earth during the period referred to.

That magnetism is an universal force is almost susceptible of demonstration. It is known to exist in
every body of matter from a crystal to the sun.
Plucker found that the axis of crystallization "tended
to assume either axial or equatorial directions."
Faraday says, "all bodies exhibit signs of inductive
influence." Professor Henry * says, " the forces of
magnetism act at great distances through all inter-
posed bodies, and like gravitation diminish in intensity with the square of the distance."

Since, then, this is the case, there can be no doubt
that our hypothesis will conform to all astronomical
mathematical formulæ. At the same time it offers a
better reason for the results of spectrum analyses
than can be found in the theory that light and heat
are radiated in their phenomenal condition.

It may be asked, why has magnetic force taken so
small a place in the science of astronomy ?

I think the answer lies in the fact that gravitation
as a primary force has been over-rated ; and that the
merits of magnetism have not been fairly considered.

---

* Professor Joseph Henry, Smithsonian Institute, Washington, D. C.

# CHAPTER IV.

## NIGHT-SIDE PHENOMENA.

MAGNETIC presentation is the key to magnetic force. If two magnets are to be presented to each other, it is impossible to know what will be the effect unless we know whether their *like* or *unlike* poles are to be presented.*

If there be a magnetic connection between the earth and the sun, the first question that should arise is, What is the mode of presentation? Do they present their *like* or *unlike* poles to each other? Since we have good reasons to believe that certain phenomena are the effects of such a connection, we ought to apply the key. If we do not we may keep on guessing and perhaps never arrive at a correct conclusion.

The northern and southern aurorae (*borealis* and

---

* We should also know whether there is to be a direct polar presentation or an indirect or an equatorial one, and if either of the latter, then for accuracy the measure of its obliquity.

*australis*) are known to be the effect of such a connection. Richard A. Proctor, commenting on this
phenomenon, says:

"The longest period that has been thoroughly established
is one of about eleven years. . . . . The perturbations of
the magnetic needle undoubtedly attain their maximum extent at intervals of eleven years. . . . . Hence we infer that
the auroral action waxes and wanes in the same period. A
remarkable association also appears to exist between disturbances of the earth's magnetism and the occurrence of
spots on the sun. It has been demonstrated that the solar
spots increase and decrease in a period of about eleven years.

" A great solar outburst witnessed by Carrington and Hod-
son, September 27, 1859, was not only accompanied by extreme magnetic disturbances, but on the same day remarkable auroras occurred in both hemispheres. Telegraphic
communication was interrupted on all the principal lines;
the operators at Washington and Philadelphia received sharp
electric shocks.

"Some doubt has been thrown on the supposed connection
in consequence of the failure of observers to obtain corrobora-
tive evidence during the past thirteen years, but the connection between the solar spot period and auroral displays
has been thoroughly established."

He then proceeds with tables compiled from the
observations of Loomis and Kamptz, showing that
auroral displays occur more frequently at the equinoctial than at the solstitial periods.

Referring to the changes taking place in the direction of the magnetic-needle, Professor Henry* says :

"The second system of changes has evident relation to the position of the earth in its orbit around the sun and its revolution on its axis. These changes were at first ascribed to the influence of the heat of the sun on different parts of the earth. But they have this remarkable character of exhibiting notably the same amount in the southern hemisphere as in the northern and in the tropical as in the temperate zones. We must, therefore, ascribe the effect to the direct magnetism of the sun itself and consider it established that this luminary, like the earth, possesses attracting and repelling poles."

Further on he gives an illustration of two globes representing the earth and the sun, and says :

"It is evident that in one-half of the orbit of the moving globe the northern poles will be inclined toward each other, while in the other half the southern poles will be similarly inclined."

If Professor Henry is right about this, if the north pole of the earth is inclined toward the north pole of the sun during one-half of the year, and its south pole toward the south pole of the sun during the other half, this is an instance in which "like poles" are presented to each other all the time, and they should

---

* Professor Joseph Henry, Smithsonian Institute, Washington, D.C.

repel each other all the time. If this be not the fact, then physical laws cannot be depended on under all circumstances.

It appearing from the premises that the earth and the sun ought to repel each other, let us inquire if there be not a class of phenomena that point to the conclusion that they do repel each other.

According to our hypothesis, the northern and southern aurorae, the zodiacal light, the belts of Jupiter and its occasional square-shouldered appearance and cometic displays are produced by the repellant magnetism of the sun; and they all may be considered as cognate atmospheric phenomena.

Auroral displays have been described with great minuteness by numerous observers in both hemispheres. Their appearance is too well known to need recital. It is certain that they have a magnetic origin, and that fact, and what little is known of their periodicity, comprises all that has been learned about them.

M. de la Rive says :

"The electric discharges which take place between the positive electricity of the atmosphere and the negative electricity of the earth are the essential and unique cause of the formation of the polar light."—*Arctic Manual*, p. 742.

"Mr. Lengstrom concluded that an electric discharge

which could only be seen by means of the spectroscope was taking place on the surface of the ground all around him, and that from a distance it would appear as a faint display of aurora."—*Arctic Manual*, p. 739.

As to the tails of comets, the general idea is that they are formed out of the gaseous envelope surrounding the nucleus. It is believed, that the gases composing the envelope are, by their near approach to the sun, expanded and driven away by the intense heat of that body. But there are many if not insuperable objections to this hypothesis. Comets have been observed with fine tails when further away from the sun than the orbit of the earth. In such cases the heat from the sun ought not to have been very great, and certainly would not have been at the polar extremities of the comet. If to meet this objection, we suppose the comet to be in a heated condition, we are left to solve the problem how it became heated, and why it did not cool during its two hundred or more years' passage through space? And since they are comparatively small bodies, this is not an easy question to answer, even if we consider that interstellar space is no colder than the region five or six miles above the earth, and also assume that the comet has made but one revolution.

But the heat hypothesis is subject to still greater

objections, and one in particular, which seems con-
clusive against it. This objection lies in the fact,
that comets' tails do not follow the comets in their
wake, but are always extended at angles to their
course and sometimes at almost right angles. Now
it seems impossible for a body to be moving in an
ellipse with almost lightning speed, and at the same
time carrying a gaseous appendage extended millions
of miles at a large angle to its course. Under such
circumstances the appendage would be forced to follow in its wake, or we can place no reliance on physical principles.

The following quotation is a lucid description of
the phenomenon ; and also a forcible presentation of
the obstacles that prevent us from assuming that
comets' tails are composed of any kind of matter with
which we are acquainted.

" In no respect is the question of the materiality of the
tail more forcibly pressed on us for consideration than in
that of the enormous sweep which it makes round the sun
in perihelio, in the manner of a straight and rigid rod in de-
fiance of the laws of gravitation, nay even of the received
laws of motion, extending (as we have seen in the comet of
1680 and 1843) from near the sun's surface to the earth's
orbit, yet whirled around unbroken, in the latter case, through
an angle of 180°, in a little more than two hours. It seems
utterly incredible, that in such case it is one and the same

material object which is being brandished. If there could be conceived such a thing as a negative shadow, a momentary impression made upon the luminiferous ether behind the comet, this would represent in some degree the conception such a phenomenon calls up; but this is not all. Even such an extraordinary excitement of the ether, conceive it as we will, will afford no account of the projection of lateral streamers; of the effusion of light from the nucleus of a comet toward the sun; and its subsequent rejection of the irregular and capricious mode in which that effusion has been seen to take place; none of the clear indications of alternate evaporation and condensation going on in the immense regions of space occupied by the tail and coma—none, in short, of innumerable other facts which link themselves with almost equally irresistible cogency to our ordinary notions of matter and force."
—Herschel's *Outlines of Astronomy*, sec. 599.

From which we ought to promptly conclude that we are laboring under a fundamental error.

When we see a comet flying swiftly along its perihelion with its luminous tail extended on its right side, we are profoundly impressed with the idea that the sun is exerting toward it a repellant force. It seems as if a strong wind, proceeding from the sun, is carrying away a volume of luminous dust which by attractive force is still held attached to the nucleus. Closely observing the tail we notice that the repellant energy, whatever it may be, is very irregular or intermittent. Sometimes the tail flashes out to an immense distance, and then instantly shrinks back as if the power were slightly withdrawn. In a moment it flashes out again. The length of these flashes and subsidences can only be estimated in millions of miles. Evidently we are viewing swifter movements than can be made by any kind of matter.

An auroral display is also a night-side phenomenon. Its flashes and subsidences are also intermittent. Its streamers sometimes appear to reach the zenith and then momentarily shrink back and flash out again in precisely the same manner.

It is scarcely necessary to add that I consider the tail of a comet as an auroral display of magnificent proportions.

I am also inclined to believe that the "square-shouldered" appearance of Jupiter which certainly has been seen by some astronomers, and which has not been seen by others who have had equal opportunities,.is the effect of an auroral display on that planet. Of course we only see the day-side of Jupiter, but this would not prevent auroral protuberances at its magnetic poles from being seen at times when there was an unusually fine display. Such protuberances, seen at four places on the apparent rim of the planet, would fully account for the appearance referred to. Our hypothesis also accounts for the fact that it is only seen occasionally.

But leaving this, I believe that the forces of attraction and repulsion very nearly counterbalance each other so far as our earth is concerned, and that consequently we would have no auroral displays were it not for circumstances which I will endeavor to explain, first remarking that the conditions to be explained are not considered as peculiar to our planet.

The magnetic poles of the earth are located about the 65° of north and south latitude.* Investigation has shown that they do not extend uniformly around the earth at any geographical degree, but that they form a zigzag line around the earth, with certain points of intensity found sometimes north and sometimes south of what may be called the mean magnetic parallel. By analogy I assume that the magnetic poles of the sun form a similar zigzag line around that body near its 65° of latitude. Then if it be true or even approximately true as I have suggested, that the earth is carried around the sun by the first circuit of attractive force and at the same time firmly pressed against the mutual repellant force of their respective second circuits, the diurnal revolution of the earth

---

* Accuracy is not aimed at or necessary.

would cause the magnetic points of intensity near the earth's magnetic parallel to be constantly matching or mismatching similar points on the sun and the irregularity in both phenomena would be accounted for.

For instance, let the 65° of north latitude be the mean magnetic parallel on both earth and sun. Let a certain point of intensity be located one degree south of this mean parallel on the earth and another in a similar situation on the sun. Now it is certain that when these two points matched each other (as the diurnal revolution of both bodies would be sure in time to make them do) the actual distance between magnetic poles would be shorter than when such points matched at the 65° or 66° of latitude, and this shortened distance would represent the increased force just the same as if the bodies had been brought that number of miles nearer to each other. Now the earth does not move back to satisfy the demands of this condition. But the second circuit of the sun advances beyond the semi-diameter of the earth at the equator, and as the diameter of the earth is much less at the 65° of latitude, the counter-forces may be said to pass through the earth and some distance beyond it at the degree of latitude last mentioned. But this would not produce light on the night-side were it not for the fact that before the sun's advancing circuit reaches the surface of the night-side it comes in contact with the inside route of the earth's second circuit on that side. The effect of this is that the earth's circuit is checked and the light-producing counter-forces are thrown backward and forward along its route, forcing faint flashes of light upward on the night-side of the earth near its magnetic parallels. These are the streamers. I have seen them at the 37° north latitude reaching almost to the zenith. They have been seen quite frequently as low as the 28°, and it has been stated that an auroral display was once seen at Havana, Cuba.

Auroral displays occur more frequently during the equinoctial than during the solstitial periods. This confirms our hypothesis, the position of the earth and sun at the equinoctials being such that both north and south "like poles" are presented to each other or at least more nearly so than during the solstices.

The solar outburst witnessed by Carrington and Hodgson and the remarkable auroral displays and magnetic disturbances accompanying it occurred within a few days of the autumnal equinox. We assume that all the phenomena were the effect of a simultaneous matching of magnetic points of intensity on both hemispheres of the earth and sun.

The variation in the appearance of auroral displays is hardly worth considering. Light is the most fitful of all phenomena. How many persons if stationed at a sharp angle to a mirror could state what objects it would reflect without looking at it? We have all seen the reflection of a great fire when the fire was out of sight; and the mirage brings objects into view that we knew were below the horizon. Conclusions drawn from every-day phenomena are sufficient to account for the different appearance of the aurora.

The zodiacal light is a lenticular shaped body of light occasionally seen in moderately high latitudes after sunset and before sunrise. In low latitudes it is almost a regular nightly occurrence; near the equator it is a very brilliant phenomenon frequently seen at midnight on the eastern and western horizons simultaneously. It is generally believed to be a solar appendage ; some speculation has been indulged in as to whether it is composed of gaseous or solid matter. Proctor says :

"The most probable interpretation of the zodiacal light is that which regards it as caused by multitudes of minute bodies traveling around the sun. At the same time two points must be carefully noted. In the first place there are phenomena of the zodiacal light which indicate some resemblance between its structure and that of comets' tails. So that not only meteoric matter alone, but cometic matter also is probably present in it."—*American Cyclopædia*, article Zodiacal Light.

Why this great astronomer avoided the words gaseous matter and used the words "cometic matter" cannot be answered. It is certain that we know nothing about cometic matter as distinguished from gaseous matter.

I do not know whether all the great astronomers are agreed that the zodiacal light is a solar append-age, but I do know that there are many thoughtful persons who are not of that opinion.

I remember having read about ten or fifteen years ago, the report of a convention of "scientists" which had been held in England, in which it was stated that "an old gentleman from the interior," so the report ran, "read a paper before the convention in which he gave his reasons for believing the zodiacal light to be an atmospheric phenomenon. At the close of the reading Richard A. Proctor rose and pronounced the views advanced in the paper wholly untenable; the old gentleman made no reply." I have sometimes thought that he may have had no reason to keep silent except that he did not want to tilt with the first English astronomer of the day.

From April 2, 1853, to April 22, 1855, the Rev. George Jones, chaplain of the United States Navy, while cruising with the Japan expedition in the Pacific ocean, took 341 observations of the zodiacal light and charted each one of them  They were taken almost daily during the time mentioned.  The charts, together with his explanations and deductions, were published by the government as a supplemental report to the report of the expedition.  I will not attempt to give a synopsis of the work; nothing short of the report itself can do Mr. Jones justice; one has only to read it to be convinced that he was an able, conscientious, careful investigator.  Moreover he was an unbiased observer, as fully appears in the report.

Mr. Jones notices the intermittent character of the light, and he also describes a swelling out, both laterally and upward, of the pyramid with an increased brightness of the light, and then "in a few minutes a shrinking back of the pyramid and a dimming of the light and so back and forth for three-quarters of an hour."

This indefatigable observer came to the conclusion that the zodiacal light is a ring of matter surrounding the earth.  His opinion was, that the apparent changes of the location of the phenomenon, as seen from different stations not widely separated, pointed conclusively to the fact that it is a ring of nebulous matter *located relatively near the earth, and certainly within the moon's orbit.*

He cites some cases in which he thought the moon was the cause of the phenomenon, and when referring to these cases says : " For myself, I have no doubt that what I saw in the cases given was really *zodiacal light produced by the moon.*"

Mr. Jones knew that in recording the fact that he had seen the " zodiacal light produced by the moon," he was placing himself in direct opposition to the solar appendage theory, and also to the conclusions of many learned astronomers. Therefore, he remarks, " There was no subject connected with these observations which I so carefully watched."

He also endeavors to show that his idea of a " nebulous ring surrounding the earth " is in harmony with the nebular hypotheses and in this connection says :

"This great theory of Laplace, called his nebular hypothesis, appears to be looked upon by astronomers with wonder, almost with awe; and as a theory which they may scarcely dare to touch. Although it is regarded with favor, yet there are few cosmologists who venture a decided opinion upon it, and while there are few points from which it can be controverted, Laplace himself seems to have exhausted what can be said in its favor in the few lines which he has given to it in a manner far from positive and in a retired corner of his book. If the theory be true, however, we have reason to think that no one of the planets may have absorbed in itself all the nebulous matter of the ring from which it was originally formed; and that consequently there may be to each of them a remainder substance in the form of a ring or rings with the planet for its centre. In the case of Saturn such rings are visible by the aid of our glasses. To Jupiter such rings have given four satellites; for our own globe one satellite has been produced and we may well query whether there may not be still a remainder of the nebulous matter left from the ring originally producing the earth; the nebulous substance of that ring not having been all exhausted in the formation of our earth and its moon and showing itself in a ring such as we are now considering."

As the third paragraph of Mr. Jones' " deductions " is in opposition to the hypotheses herein to be presented, we quote it in full, leaving the reader to determine whether the reason given is sufficient to warrant the conclusion drawn.

" *This light cannot be a reflection from our atmosphere* taking its shape from that; for the atmosphere though brought doubtless by the axial motion of the earth into a somewhat lenticular shape, must have its elongation directly over the earth's equator; and the course of the zodiacal light shows not the slightest affinity to the equatorial line."

Mr. Proctor, commenting on Mr. Jones observations and conclusions, says:

"But it is certain that no ring surrounding the earth could possibly explain the phenomena of the zodiacal light when they are all considered together, however competent to explain the particular phenomena observed by Mr. Jones. It is to be noted in particular that the phenomena observed in high latitudes, though not so striking as those observed in low latitudes, are in reality even more instructive. It will be manifest if there were a ring surrounding the earth at a distance so moderate that a traveler in tropical regions could recognize the zodiacal change of position as he passed from the northern to the southern side of the equator it would be invisible from places in high latitude. This is clearly shown in the writer's treatise on Saturn where the configuration of the rings viewed from the different Saturnian latitudes has been carefully calculated, not merely surmised from general considerations."—*American Cyclopædia*, article Zodiacal Light.

It seems to me that the great astronomer misapprehended Mr. Jones, not as to his conclusions, but as to the facts. It was not a *" particular phenomena "* that Mr. Jones had been observing. He scoured the ocean while engaged in the work for about 6000 miles north and south and 15,000 miles east and west. He made three hundred and forty-one charts exhibiting the structure of the light as it appeared to him at morning, evening and midnight at the different stations on his route. It was the zodiacal light that he was observing. If he did not see the general phenomenon he was a very unlucky man.

Mr. Jones does not say that the phenomenon he saw

at 53° 30′ south latitude could have been seen at 41° 32′ north latitude, nor does he intimate that the same zodiacal light can be seen across 93° of latitude. He simply records the fact that he witnessed it at both situations, and in common with other writers on the subject he undoubtedly supposed there was but one ring.

If the zodiacal light is a ring of matter surrounding the earth it could be seen at high latitudes if it is sufficiently elevated. On the other hand, if it is a ring surrounding the sun, it ought to be a constant phenomenon at the 45° of latitude.

Again the statement that Mr. Jones' conclusions were "*surmised from general considerations*" is opposed to the record. His charts represent a degree of ability fully equal to the work. He supports his theory by careful calculations based on well-chosen data. He had the advantage of Mr. Proctor in this, that he was not calculating the distance of a phenomenon several hundred million miles away, but one so near that *its apparent place changed because of the ship's progress in a single night.*

As to conclusions drawn from Saturn's rings or from calculations based on their "*configuration when viewed from the different Saturnian latitudes,*" they are very interesting. But that planet is about eight times farther from us than the sun, sixteen times farther than the planet Mars. In round numbers, Saturn is about 800,000,000 miles from us, and its greatest diameter is less than 75,000 miles. We may suppose that an error amounting to a very small fraction of a hair's breadth would alter the result of any calculation thousands of miles. However this may be, I think 780,000,000 miles is too far to bring a witness, not to corroborate an hypothesis, but to dispute the facts of our home phenomena.

With Mr. Jones' three hundred and forty-one charts lying before me, I do not hesitate to say that either the facts apparent on the face of them must be refuted, or the idea that the zodiacal light is a ring of matter surrounding the sun must be abandoned.

The depth of our atmosphere is usually estimated at from fifty to one hundred miles.* The estimates for the most part are based on the duration of twilight. No doubt they are correct as to the depth ordinarily lighted by the sun. But I venture to think that there is no essential difference in the component parts of the gaseous medium lying between the earth and the sun. That it simply becomes more tenuous in an outward direction from the earth and

---

* Some persons think that extremely rarefied portions of it extend upward five hundred miles.

denser again at the neighborhood of the sun. I am aware that the ancient philosophers believed in an universal ether and that modern physicists have found its existence necessary to enable them to explain the diffractions, polarizations and interferences of light. But as said before, light is a capricious phenomenon, and, therefore, deductions from it or from any of its manifestations are not to be depended upon with the same assurance as those derived from other sources.

If the density of our atmosphere continues to decrease as rapidly as it does for the first five or six miles, there must be comparatively near to us a gaseous medium sufficiently tenuous to allow the heavenly bodies to move in their orbits apparently not at all resisted. And this would certainly be the case if such medium is unable to exhibit any noticeable phenomena except when excited by the counter-forces of two large magnetic bodies of matter more than ordinarily out of equilibrium.

However, it is evident that the solar rays, whether they be light and heat rays or currents of magnetic force, do not usually light the atmosphere higher than one hundred miles. I think this is not because the rarer medium is unable to perform light vibrations, but because it requires an extraordinary degree of force to make it do so. Indeed, the cometic phe-

nomena furnish strong indications that the most
tenuous medium in space can perform such vibrations whenever the binary magnetic forces are operating in it with sufficient intensity.

I think the reason our atmosphere is not lighted
higher, lies in our hypothesis that the earth's third
circuit, being simply a dynamic expression, is not ordinarily strong enough to produce the necessary
vibration higher than the distances mentioned.

I believe that the forces of the first and second circuits of every heavenly body pass through space without causing any noticeable phenomena until they
reach some other large body and then their third circuits rise and our senses recognize phenomena which
are their natural counterpart.

I do not mean that "atoms" or molecules of
matter have no third circuits. I am only speaking of that degree of phenomena recognized by our
senses.

In short, I believe that the light and heat recognized by us, are confined to the region in which our
third circuit acts with sufficient power to aid in their
production, and that the height to which it acts is an
exponent of the distance the solar and earthly poles
are separated. That when there is a matching of the
nearer points of intensity, our third circuit rises on

the night-side, and when such is not the case it rises higher on the day-side.*

In like manner and for the same reasons the solar third circuit is not ordinarily strong enough to aid in the production of noticeable light farther away from the surface of the sun than perhaps 10,000 or 15,000 miles. Outside of the action of great third circuits, I believe space is everywhere dark and cold.

The second circuits are supposed to contend with each other throughout our solar system. We cannot say throughout the universe, because infinite space cannot be contemplated as an entirety.

The sun, with an atmosphere from 10,000 to 15,-000 miles deep, may have a finer climate than the earth, for it does not follow that its atmosphere would be any heavier on account of its depth, the latter being simply a measurement of magnetic repulsion, *i.e.*, an expression of solar equilibrium. And on general principles, all things conform to the usual condi-

---

* I am of the opinion that the "copper-colored" appearance of the moon seen when it is totally eclipsed, is due to the magnetic relationship existing between it and the earth, and not to the light reflected from our atmosphere. Our earth presents its night-side to the moon during a lunar eclipse. And what is called "the new moon in the old moon's arms," I account for in the same manner.

tion of the forces and effects around and about
them.

The light and heat received by the sun on account
of its connection with the earth must be considered
with reference to its condition. We cannot say
that it receives as much as we receive from it,
yet the effect may be just as beneficent in every
respect.

Before proceeding further with our inquiry as to the
origin and nature of the zodiacal light, it becomes necessary to note the condition of our atmosphere conform-
able to our hypothesis. It is clear that it must be regarded as a residuum of primordial matter. Hence its
particles should assume on the different parts of the
earth the same inclination and declination assumed by
the magnetic needle, that is, horizontal at the magnetic equator and perpendicular at the magnetic
parallels and at the poles. Being arranged as stated,
the earth is attracting them and they are attracting
each other vertically at the magnetic poles and repelling each other laterally; while at the magnetic
equator the earth is repelling them and they are repelling each other vertically and attracting each other
north and south. (See Fig. 10.) This ought to cause
the atmosphere to be deeper, *i.e.*, denser at a greater
height at the magnetic equator than at the poles.

The effect of this on atmospheric tides and aerial phenomena cannot be estimated.

The effect of the sun's magnetism on our atmosphere is the same, whether we consider it attractive or repellant. To estimate it, however, is a difficult problem, not so much on account of its tangential character, but on account of our ignorance of the manner in which a gaseous body moves when under the influence of such forces. Therefore, we are compelled to theorize.

If a sea of nearly uniform depth encompassed the earth, sound reasoning would lead us to conclude that the attractive force of the sun at the time of an equinox would cause an elevation of the water near the equator, and that diurnal revolution would prolong the elevation into an equatorial belt. When the apparent course of the sun ran north, portions of this belt would break off and follow it. When the rays of the sun became vertical at the Tropic of Cancer, there would be an elevated belt near that parallel. When the sun started south, portions of this tropical belt would follow it, the loss being supplied by a flow from the north. This would make these belts *somewhat* permanent, but not of uniform depth even considered hourly.

Again, when the sun is vertical at the equator, the

greatest tangential effect of its attraction is at the poles. But as the sun changes its position, the polar tangents change theirs, so that when the sun's rays are vertical at the Tropic of Capricorn the northern tangent is at the Arctic Circle and the southern beyond the south pole.

The tangential effect east and west need not be taken into consideration, as it is for the most part overcome by diurnal revolution.

A little reflection on this shifting of the attractive force, leads to the conclusion that there would be in our imaginary sea an elevated belt at the equator, and one at each of the tropics, and another at each of the arctic circles.*

Of these belts the equatorial would be the most permanent; the tropical somewhat stable, and the arctic if they exist at all, would be inconstant and very irregular in form.

---

* These belts not being the effect of centrifugal force, but of the attraction of the sun, their location would correspond very nearly to the ecliptic. Mr. Jones says: "*A plane passing through the centre of the zodiacal light as it shows itself through the varying latitudes of these observations would correspond pretty nearly with the ecliptic;* but how near the two planes approach to a coincidence, it seems to be yet impossible to say."

The fragmentary belts following the sun would of course extend from east to west in a general way, yet sometimes the eastern and sometimes the western end of them would first leave the main belt. This would give them an inclination which would probably not be very greatly changed until they were absorbed in the general flow.

We have assumed the elevation of the water to be the effect of the sun's attraction ; at the same time, we must bear in mind that the belts are the effect of the diurnal revolution of the earth, and since the day-side of the earth is constantly becoming its night-side, the general result is precisely the same, whether the force be attractive or repellant.

Now let the force be repellant, and let the supposed sea be the real atmosphere. Then, when portions of the atmosphere break from the belts they should follow the sun with considerable regularity, and this they certainly would do if the force involved were as uniform as the force of gravity. I have endeavored to show that the force is not uniform, but is subject to daily, hourly, and momentary pulses of magnetic intensity. The result of which is that while the belts are following the sun* in a general way they are

---

* Mr. Jones's records on the zodiacal light read as follows : "Through July of 1854, the apices in the evening were de-

liable to be, and often are set forward or backward as the pressure is increased or diminished. The barometric " highs" and " lows" indicate the passage of these fragmentary belts over the land, when by increased or diminished pressure they are rapidly driven forward or set back, waves of different temperature are forced together and condensation and precipitation are the result. At such times storms are frequent and barometric changes take place rapidly ; moreover the molecules composing the warmer cloud-masses within the belts form local circuits in which the force is moving in a certain direction. If these meet with colder masses in which the force is moving in the same direction they coalesce, *i.e.*, establish an equilibrium without any phenomenal disturbance. But they are just as likely to meet with similar circuits charged with opposing currents, and when this occurs, both circuits are instantly broken up, and the freed force descends with a flash of light to the earth where it is

---

cidedly on the northern side of the elliptic though my latitude was only about 25° north; while in September of the same year though my latitude was nearly as before, the apices were on the southern side." He also notices that the zodiacal light and the ecliptic quite frequently cross each other. In short his observations conclusively show that the light is by no means a stationary phenomenon.

converted into heat; the latter being simply another expression of the same thing.

It may be asked whether there be any analogies supporting the hypothesis in so far as it relates to the belts.

I am of the opinion that the belts of Jupiter corroborate the hypothesis; I am willing to believe that since we find atmospheric belts on his surface, we may find similar ones on some of the other planets if we are looking for them.*    That whether we do or not, we may find better evidence of their existence here at home where we have admitted the possibility.

I am willing to go further and believe that the form of Jupiter's belts may, in a general way, represent the form of the earth's belts.

Herschel says:

"The disc of Jupiter is always observed to be crossed in one direction by dark bands or belts presenting the appearance in Plate III. Fig. 2; which represents this planet as seen on the 23d of September, 1832, in the twenty feet reflector of Slough.    These belts are, however, by no means

---

* Other planets may not have belts.    Jupiter undoubtedly has a very deep atmosphere.    Also the inclination of his axis is only about 3°, and since the force involved is sometimes greater and sometimes less, the condition of Jupiter is very favorable to belt formation.

alike at all times; they vary in breadth and in situation on the disc (though never in their general direction). They have been seen broken up and distributed over the whole face of the planet ; but this phenomenon is extremely rare. Branches running out from them, and subdivisions as represented in the figure, as well as evident dark spots are by no means uncommon."—*Outlines of Astronomy*, sec. 512.

FIG. 11.

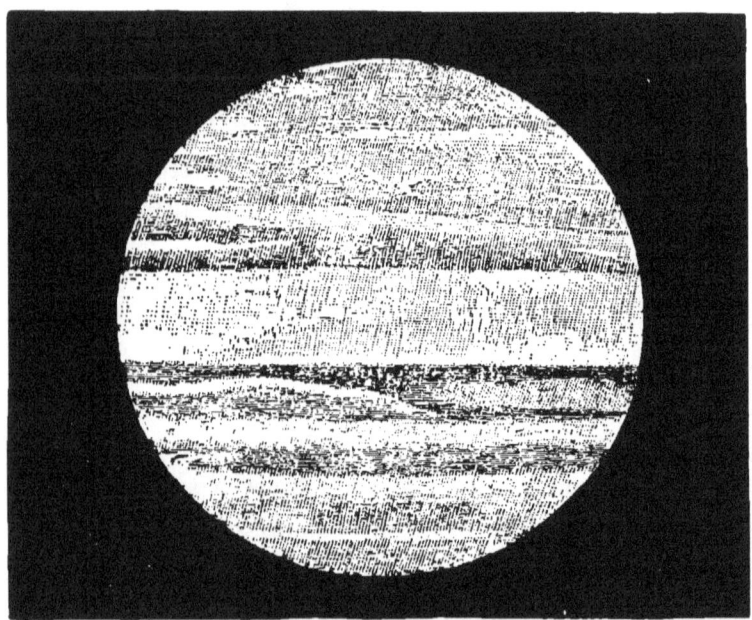

Jupiter's Belts.

Our Figures 11 and 12 represent the usual appearance of Jupiter as seen in powerful telescopes; the lighter portions of their discs correspond to the deeper portions of his atmosphere. We notice that a fragmentary belt has broken from the south tropical belt and is apparently moving north to join the equatorial belt. A similar but not so well defined fragment has parted from the equatorial belt and is moving north to join the north tropical belt. Compare these figures with any good sketch of this planet made at a time when the belt formations were well defined.

Fig. 12.

Jupiter's Belts.

As we ascend mountains the temperature of the atmosphere decreases about one degree for every 300 or 400 feet, and its density diminishes at about the same rate. From which we learn that it is deeper above the valley than above the mountains. Let the mountains be our barometer and examine their testimony. At the equator perpetual frost is found at an elevation of about 15,000 feet, at the 60° north latitude it is found at about 4000 feet. From this we are not to infer that the depth of the atmosphere varies to that extent; nor need we suppose that its depth is the principal cause, but it is certainly one of the causes and it may be a more important one than we have considered it.

One is apt to think that as we proceed north or south from the equator, the perpetual frost line creeps down the mountain sides with considerable regularity and that the irregularities that do occur are the effect of different exposures to the rays of the sun, or of humidity and other local causes. But even guarded in this way the assumption does not meet the case.

The following table (p. 121) of frost line observances is taken from Olmsted's *Philosophy* revised by Snell. It is an old work but a very good one.

We notice that in the first five degrees the frost line falls only 122 feet; in the second, 388; in the third, 569; in the fourth, 779; so far it falls with considerable uniformity. But in the next five degrees there seems to be some disturbing cause at work; the line only falls 689 feet, which is less than it fell in the preceding period. Then from the twenty-fifth

to the thirtieth degrees, as if the cause had been suddenly removed, it plunges down 1438 feet, more than
double the distance it fell in the preceding period.

| Latitude. | Altitude. | Difference for each 5°. |
|:---:|:---:|:---:|
| 0 | 15,557 | ...... |
| 5 | 15,455 | 122 |
| 10 | 15,067 | 388 |
| 15 | 14,498 | 569 |
| 20 | 13,719 | 779 |
| 25 | 13,030 | 689 |
| 30 | 11,592 | 1438 |
| 35 | 10,664 | 928 |
| 40 | 9,016 | 1648 |
| 45 | 7,658 | 1358 |
| 50 | 6,260 | 1398 |
| 55 | 4,912 | 1348 |
| 60 | 3,684 | 1228 |
| 65 | 2,516 | 1168 |
| 70 | 1,577 | 959 |
| 75 | 748 | 809 |
| 80 | 120 | 628 |

We may say that observations of this kind are not
to be implicitly relied on; that the uniformity may
have been broken by some of the local causes re-

ferred to.  Yet, when we remember that the tropical
lines are located near the centre of the five degrees in
which the irregularity is found, the facts leave a strong
impression on the mind that the cause of the irregularity is not local.

Now bringing our knowledge of the earth's con-
vexity to bear on the facts, we realize that between
the twentieth and twenty-fifth degrees of latitude,
there is a belt of atmosphere which, inasmuch as it
fails to conform to the configuration of the earth,
may be said to be an elevated belt.

It is probable that the table does not comprise a
great number of observations, particularly in the very
high latitudes.  No doubt, they were all taken within
the periods in which they are tabulated, yet greater
numbers may have been taken higher or lower in
them, and therefore the data would be more satisfactory if the observations had been arranged in degrees.

I do not claim that these observations strikingly
corroborate the atmospheric belt hypothesis, but I
do claim, that they indicate the probability of such
belts at or near the tropics, and the possibility of
lower ones at or near the arctic circles, but the magnetic arrangement of the atmospheric molecules, may
prevent any noticeable rise at the localities last mentioned.

Applying the appearance of Jupiter's belts to the supposed belts of the earth it becomes necessary to remember, that we are observing Jupiter's belts spread out in their respective situations apparently in low relief, while the spectator of the zodiacal light is observing the crest of the belt then producing the phenomenon.

I consider that the zodiacal light is caused by precisely the same magnetic conditions which cause the auroral displays; with this difference, that in the latter the counter-forces (by reason of the smallness of the earth's diameter at the auroral locations) rise high above the earth's central night-side. While in the case of the zodiacal light the greater diameter of the earth prevents them from doing so. Hence the zodiacal light is seen on the eastern or western horizon and when there is a very fine display it may be seen at midnight on both horizons. Moreover, in an auroral display the counter-forces are emanating from the earth under the feet of the arctic traveler, while in the zodiacal light the earth's night-side second circuit is not brought into such close contact with the solar circuit.

To avoid being misunderstood I will repeat. Our atmosphere is not considered as having an upper surface in the ordinary sense. The supposition is that all the rarer medium, however tenuous it may be, is able to exhibit luminous phenomena, such as we are able to recognize whenever the counterforces of two magnetic bodies of sufficient strength are operating in it.

For instance, if we suppose the earth suddenly brought 10,000 miles nearer the sun, the northern and southern auroræ would rise correspondingly high on its night-side, and the zodiacal light would also rise; and that if the earth could then be seen in perspective it would appear to have five luminous tails, perhaps seven.

My idea is that a comet's tail is not composed of the comet's atmosphere except to a very limited extent. It is the forces that have extended their sway and the universal atmosphere is responding to them. In other words, vibrations have proceeded outwardly from the comet and *vibration is light.*

No doubt some of the comet's atmosphere is piled up, so to speak, on its night-side. But let us not forget that the tremendous attractive force of the comet is acting on its own atmosphere at its poles, and so holding its own against the increased repulsion at the magnetic poles and at the equator, and hence we see the comet's atmosphere peeling off from its day-side, passing to its night-side and to its poles. In this manner the individuality of the comet is maintained while we are observing it, and since it may be rotating hourly or even momentarily the phenomenon is a very peculiar one.

If the premises be true, we learn that a comet's local attractive force, derived from its first circuit attachment to the universe, preserves it from being dissipated into space, while its own second and third circuits, enable it to leave the dangerous proximity into which it has been brought.

Accordingly there is no movement of material except that taking place near the nucleus. The great tail that extended for millions of leagues and swept through an arc of 180° in two hours was nothing but a luminous impression; the sensate effect of increased vibration taking place in the interstellar atmosphere as the triple counter-forces swept through it.

I consider that comet's tails are no more substantial than the reflection of light thrown from a mirror. Herschel likened them to "*negative shadows.*" What can negative shadows be but rays of light?

In his description of the tails he says :

"Stars of the smallest magnitude remain distinctly visible, though covered by what appears to be the densest portion of the substance, although the same would be completely obliterated by a moderate fog extending only a few yards above the surface of the earth."—*Outlines of Astronomy*, sec. 558.

Dwelling on the same subject, he says:

"That the luminous tail of a comet is something in the nature of a smoke, fog or cloud suspended in a transparent atmosphere, is evident from a fact which has often been noticed, viz., that the portion of the tail where it comes up and surrounds the head *is yet separated from it* by an interval less luminous, as if sustained by a transparent stratum, as we often see one layer of clouds over another, with a considerable clear space between them."—*Outlines of Astronomy*, sec. 560.

From this description we learn that there is an un-lighted region lying between the base of the tail and the nucleus. Here again the facts corroborate our hypothesis. In an auroral display there is also an unlighted region between the earth and the base of the luminous phenomenon.

In Chambers' *Encyclopædia* we read:

"The appearance of the aurora borealis has been described by a great variety of observers, both in northern and central Europe, all of whom give substantially the same account of the manner in which the phenomenon takes place. It is briefly as follows: A dingy aspect of the sky in the direction of the north is generally the precursor of the aurora: and this generally becomes darker in color, and assumes the form of a circular segment surrounded by a luminous arch and resting at each end on the horizon. This dark segment, as it is called, has the appearance of a thick cloud, and is frequently seen as such in the fading twilight, before the development of the auroral light. Its density, however, must be very small, as stars are sometimes seen shining brightly through it."

In a general description of comets and their movements, Herschel says :

"Their variations in apparent size during the time they continue visible are no less remarkable than those of their velocity ; sometimes they make their first appearance as faint and slow moving objects, with little or no tail, but by degrees accelerate, enlarge and throw out from them this appendage, which increases in length and brightness till (as always happens in such cases) they approach the sun and are lost in his beams. After a time they again emerge on the other side, receding from the sun with a velocity at first rapid, but gradually decaying. It is for the most part after thus passing the sun, that they shine forth in all their splendor and that their tails acquire their greatest length and development, thus indicating plainly the action of the sun's rays as the exciting cause of that extraordinary emanation. As they continue to recede from the sun, their motion diminishes and the tail dies away or is absorbed into the head, which itself grows continually feebler, and is at length altogether lost sight of in by far the greater number of cases, never to be seen more."—*Outlines of Astronomy*, sec. 561.

We think a reasonable explanation of the variations and other peculiarities mentioned by Herschel can be gathered from our chapter on world formation. However, it may not be amiss to briefly review the subject.

In the first place, the orbits of comets are in the form of ellipses, but they are not true ellipses, because of the vortical manner in which the bodies in them move. Comets approach and leave the sun as if they were following the periphery of a funnel, that is to say at a spiral angle to the sun's axis; from which it arises, that they offer to the sun attractive presentation at their aphelion, repellant presentation at their perihelion, and equilibrial presentation at their equinoxes. Therefore, their tails should be extended toward the sun in the first case, away from it in the second, and there should be no tail in the third case, and probably would not be were it not for the matching and mismatching of magnetic points of intensity heretofore mentioned and described.

If comets could get to their perihelion passages with their unlike poles presented to the sun, they would immediately coalesce with that body. But that is impossible, since the power that is propelling them in their orbits, is the same power that maintains the stability of their axial direction.

A thing much more likely to occur is the meeting of an arctic and an antarctic comet near the plane of the sun's equator (Fig. 13). In such case the vortical character of the movement would be neutralized. What would be the result can only be conjectured. It is not unreasonable to suppose that such collisions have taken place and have been the cause of many meteoric showers.

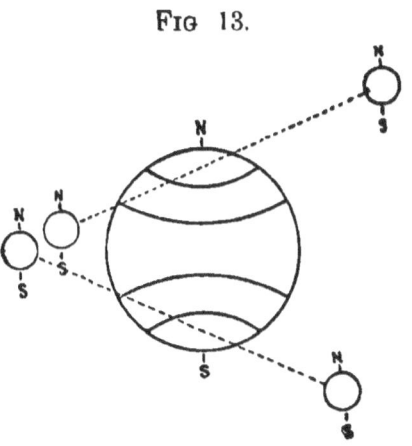

Fig 13.

Arctic and Antarctic Comets.

Assuming as we do that the orbits of comets are spiral, we notice first that a small segment of such an orbit seen at a distance would represent the hyperbolic form; then reflecting on the fact that the bodies moving in these orbits are repelled at their nearest approach and attracted at their farthest departure, and duly considering the nature of vortical motion, we arrive at the conclusion that a comet leaving the sun in hyperbola may, nevertheless, return.

There is another feature of the cometic phenomenon which Herschel describes as follows:

9

"The tails of comets are often somewhat curved bending in general toward the region which the comet has left as if moving somewhat more slowly or as if retarded in their course."—*Outlines of Astronomy*, sec. 557.

The cause of this curvature is as obscure as any part of the phenomenon. It may be the effect of the difference in time required by the light to reach us from the nearer or more distant parts of the tail. Sometimes the nucleus may have been millions of miles nearer to us than the end of the tail; at other times the reverse may have been the case. It requires time for light to travel 41,000,000 leagues.

Although magnetism is an universal force, yet its course is impeded by our atmosphere, and it may also be in some measure impeded by the universal atmosphere. Evidently it is impedition that causes the tail to become fainter and fainter till the end is reached. No doubt the forces extend far beyond the end of the tail.

Even if we were compelled to assume that the forces are slightly carried aside from their lateral course by the swiftness of their passage through a comparatively stable medium, the assumption would not be antagonistic to physical principles. And that is more than can be said of any theory in which the tails are assumed to be composed of any kind of material with which we are acquainted.

To say that *" cometic matter may be present in the zodiacal light "* amounts to no more than to say that zodiacal matter may be present in a comet's tail. The information is not worth the paper it is written on. Besides the statement is misleading, inasmuch as it conveys the idea that the writer knows something about that which he knows nothing about. Moreover, such statements leave a false impression on the mind that philosophers are acquainted with material which is neither gaseous, aqueous, or solid, and which is therefore not subject to the physical laws. This is undoubtedly the character of "cometic matter" and that of "universal ether" also, in all probability. Therefore, I am of the opinion that both these inventions are obstacles to the advance of science.

# CHAPTER V.

## THE SOLAR ENIGMA.

It is conjectured by philosophers that the sun is an incandescent body of matter, and that it has been radiating light and heat throughout the solar system for millions of years past and that it will be so engaged for ages to come. Then, since we cannot imagine a distance so great that solar light would not reach us if we had telescopes of sufficient power, we may include the universe in the supposition and infer that all the heavenly bodies are engaged in the same work. It is also supposed that the sun is at the same time growing larger by the acquisition of meteoric matter and showers of "cosmical dust."

If these conjectures be true, then matter is now and always has been gathering and centralizing in certain localities while vibrations have been proceeding outward to fill up the vacancies. This is **an** amazing, strange procedure. One is led to inquire what will be the state of sidereal affairs when the work is finished and matter shall occupy certain places in the universe and forceful phenomena shall have gone elsewhere.

The mean distance of the sun from the earth is estimated at 91,000,000 miles. Its diameter at 853-000 miles, or about one hundred and seven times the diameter of the earth, so that the body of the sun exceeds in size that of the earth 1,200,000 times. From this and telescopical observations of the solar surface, it has been inferred that the body of the sun is for the most part in a gaseous condition. This inference is mainly drawn from the sun's supposed specific gravity. It is no doubt well founded if we can rely on the theory that gravitation is the motive power that controls the machinery of the heavens.

All our ideas of weight are derived from examples of the manner in which the earth attracts detached portions of itself to itself. Ounces, pounds and tons are simply measures of the attractive force that holds the earth together, *i.e.*, prevents its materials from dissipating into space. Hence our scales express nothing more than comparative measures of the earth's inherent cohesiveness. The earth itself cannot be weighed, neither can the sun. Such bodies are too nearly in equilibrium to sustain any relation to avoirdupois.

Weight, in a certain sense, is doubtless common to all matter, and the attraction of gravity, which is another name for the same thing, may be universal. But that "law of action" usually ascribed to it and stated thus, "*the force with which two material particles respectively attract each other is directly proportioned to their mass*," is not an universal law by any means, inasmuch as it cannot be depended on even in the ordinary experiments of life. Therefore, it is no law at all, but only a convenient fallacy. A good magnet weighing two ounces will sustain a weight of three pounds and two ounces, or twenty-five times its own weight, and one of one hundred pounds will sustain two hundred and seventy-one pounds.* It is obvious that such bodies do not attract each other in direct proportion to their mass. We find all around us solid masses and fluid masses which attract and repel each other without any attempt to obey the law so stated. If it were not so the theory of molecular attraction and atomic repulsion would have no place in science. Moreover, to give the supposed law any

---

* "The magnet worn by Sir Isaac Newton weighed only 3 grains, yet it was able to lift 746 grains, or nearly 250 times its own weight. One brought from Moscow to London weighed 125 pounds, but could support only about 200 pounds."

appearance of truth, the word *mass* must be taken to mean weight, and as the attraction mentioned is alleged to be due to weight the law may be reduced to this: *That particles of matter are directly proportioned to each other according to what they respectively weigh.* The simple fact so stated hardly deserves a place in philosophy.

Therefore, when considering the sun, which we have strong reasons to believe is a magnet, we should be cautious about accepting inferences as to its physical condition unless such inference be supported by something more than its estimated weight or its supposed specific gravity.

By observations of the spots on the sun's surface, astronomers have ascertained that it rotates about an axis nearly perpendicular to the plane of the ecliptic in the same direction as the earth, that is from west to east. Its period of rotation has been estimated at twenty-five and a third days, it being the mean rotation which is meant. For there is nothing known about it except what has been learned by observing the spots on its surface, and, strange to say, they travel across the solar surface at different rates of speed, varying from twelve and two-third degrees in latitude 50° to nearly fourteen and a half degrees at the equator. From which it appears that taking two spots on the solar surface, one in latitude 45° and another on the equator, the latter will advance in longitude faster than the former, gaining daily about two degrees of longitude, so that in about one hundred and eighty days it will have gained a complete revolution; that is to say the sun's equator makes about two revolutions more per annum than the regions in 45° north and south solar latitude. It is clear from this that no reliable data can be obtained from observations of the solar surface. For it is not to be supposed that the sun is divided into three sections and that they are rotating at different rates of speed and so grinding the surfaces of each other like mill-stones. Evidently we see nothing but the atmosphere of the sun, from the movements of which we can expect to obtain but little more information than can be had from watching the smoke ascending from a tobacco-pipe. We may, however, infer this much, that since the atmosphere of the sun is carried forward in rotation faster at the solar equator than at the higher solar latitudes, there is a probability that our atmosphere may be subject to the same apparent eccentricity.

Even if the solar atmosphere were out of the way, it is almost if not entirely certain that we can learn nothing about the physical or topographical condition of that body by telescopical observations.* Any one who has seen a mountain at a distance of one hundred miles, will accept this conclusion without evidence.

Herschel says :

" A single second of angular measure corresponds on the sun's disc to 461 miles, and a circle of this diameter (containing therefore 167,000 square miles) is the least space which can be distinctly discerned on the sun as a *visible area.*"— *Outlines of Astronomy*, sec. 386.

That is to say, an area on the sun's surface nearly four times as large as Pennsylvania, can only be noticed as a mere dot.

Here, then, is a fine field for speculation, into which all who are so inclined may enter, nor need any hesitate, even on account of ignorance, for all that is known or conjectured of the sun may be learned in a couple of hours, and the facts and conjectures are proportioned to each other much the same as Falstaff's bread to his sack. Nor is it at all likely that anything more chimerical will be advanced than can be found in the common school books.

Section 10, Lockyer's *Elements of Astronomy*, reads as follows :

---

* We know very little about the physical condition of the moon although it is 379 times nearer to us than the sun.

"Now why do the stars and sun shine? They shine *because they are white hot;* they are globes of the fiercest fire; on their surfaces masses of metals and other substances are burning together more fiercely than anything we can imagine."

Herschel says:

"An easy calculation, founded on our experimental knowledge of the properties of air and the mechanical laws which regulate its dilatation and compression, is sufficient to show that at an altitude above the earth not exceeding the hundredth part of its diameter the tenuity or rarefaction of the air must be so excessive that not only animal life could not subsist or combustion be maintained in it, but the most delicate means we possess of ascertaining the existence of *any air at all* would fail to afford the slightest perceptible indications of its presence."—*Outlines of Astronomy,* sec. 33.

In the above quotation, Herschel is explaining the certainties of science. Then how can such a conflagration as Lockyer describes be maintained? Have we any reason to think that the sun is provided with a deeper atmosphere than the earth, the size of each taken into consideration? Can we think of a body of coal eight feet in diameter surrounded with an atmosphere not exceeding one inch deep, and suppose it to be in a state of combustion?

We will read again from the *Elements of Astronomy,* sec. 123:

" When the sun is totally eclipsed . . . . its atmosphere
is then seen to contain red masses of fantastic shapes; to
these the name of *red flames* and *prominences* have been given.
Now as these bodies appear much brighter than the surrounding atmosphere, we conclude that they are hotter, as a
bright fire is hotter than a dim one."

During a total eclipse of the sun the denser part
of its atmosphere is behind the moon, therefore the
comparison must be made between the red-flames and
the outside tenuous medium. It is quite probable
that the red flames are a little warmer than interstellar space, but if any great degree of heat is meant
there is very little to support the inference. Many
things are brighter than others without being hotter.
Besides we have a home phenomenon that points to a
different conclusion. Our northern and southern auroræ frequently resemble red flames which if seen in
perspective, at a distance of a few thousand miles might
appear as prominences on the rim of the earth's disc.
Yet, these earthly red flames have not sufficient heat
in them to sensibly affect the arctic atmosphere.

Judging from sketches made by those who have
observed total eclipses of the sun through powerful
telescopes, we believe that no two of them will agree
as to the appearance of the phenomenon at the same
moment of time.

Fig. 14 represents the appearance of the total solar eclipse that occurred December 22, 1870. Our figure is a copy of an engraving after a sketch made

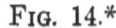

by Professor J. R. Eastman, who was one of the corps of astronomers sent by the Naval Department of the United States to the island of Sicily to observe the phenomenon. The engraving is a part of Professor Eastman's official report. The reader will observe that there may have been something like

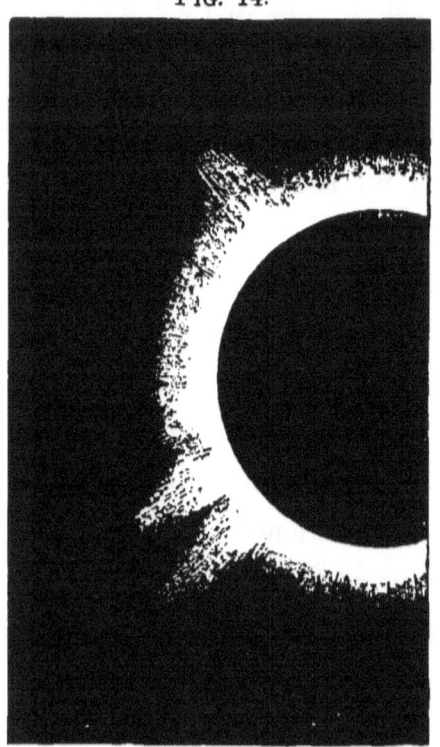

Total Eclipse of the Sun, Dec. 22, 1870.

a solar auroral display underway at the time of the eclipse.

Fig. 15 represents the eclipse as seen by Captain G. L. Tupman at the same time and place; again

---

* In the original engravings there are noticeable phenomena which cannot be shown without the aid of colored plates.

Professor Eastman says in his report, "The third and

the artist pictures something like an auroral display.

Professor Lockyer's description of the sun spots and his conclusions reads as follows:

"Some of the spots cover millions of square miles; others are visible only in power- ful instruments and are of very short duration. There is a great difference in the number of spots visible from time to time; indeed, there is a *minimum period* when none are seen for weeks together, and a *maximum period* when more are seen than at other times. The interval between two maximum or two minimum periods is about eleven years. Now as we must get less light from the sun when it is covered with spots than when it is free from them, we may look upon it as *a variable star with a period of eleven*

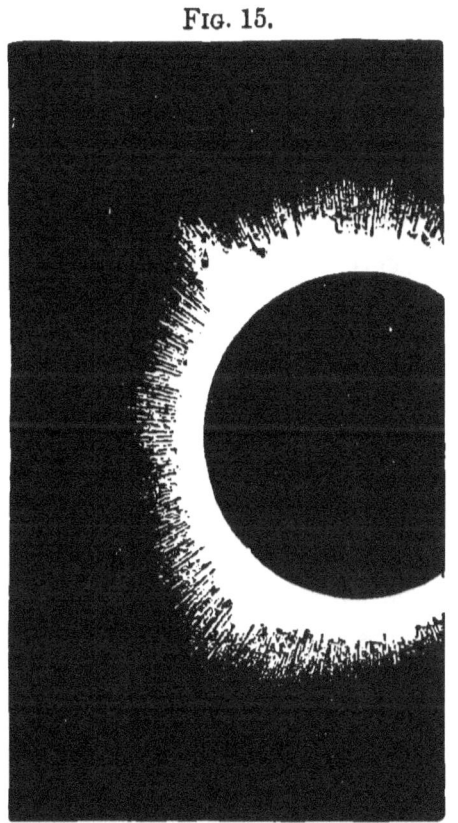

FIG. 15.

Total Eclipse of the Sun, Dec. 22, 1870.

outer portion of the corona, on the western limb of the sun consisted of three projections of light striated or of radial

*years.* . . . . It is also known that the magnetic needle has a period of the same length, its oscillations occurring when there are most sun spots. Auroræ and the currents of electricity which traverse the earth's surface are affected by a similar period. There seems, therefore, some connection between these things and the solar spots, though what it is we do not know."—*Elements of Astronomy*, sec. 125.

Then, as our auroræ have a maximum and minimum period of the same length, we may also look upon the *earth as a variable star with a period of eleven years.* We are not situated so that we can perspectively view the earth as a planet in space, hence we cannot say that it has *such spots* on its surface, but we may infer that it has.

The same author says:

"The heat thrown out from every square yard of the sun's surface is greater than that which would be produced by burning six tons of coal on it every hour. Now we may take the surface of the sun roughly at 2,284,000,000,000 square miles, and there are 3,097,600 square yards in each square mile. How many tons of coal must be burned, therefore, in an hour

---

structure, resembling the short bands of streamers that are frequently seen rising from the auroral arch. One of these projections on the northwest limb of the sun was quite small, extending not more than five minutes above the limit of the second portion of the corona. The others, one on the southwest and one on the northwest limit of the sun, attained an altitude of about nine minutes above the second division of the corona."

to represent the sun's heat?"—*Elements of Astronomy*, sec. 129.

According to the nebular hypothesis there never has been a time when coal could have been formed in the sun, and if the professor's philosophy be true, there never will be. If we are not mistaken, coal is formed from a precedent vegetation. When the sun, a body of melted vaporized metals, shall have been cooled sufficiently for vegetation to spring up, where is the heavenly body that will furnish it light and heat and all that these imply?

Further on the Professor says :

"The *whole* heat of the sun collected on a mass of ice as large as the earth would be sufficient to melt it in two minutes, to boil the water thus produced in two minutes more and turn it all into steam in a quarter of an hour from the time it was first applied."—*Elements of Astronomy*, sec. 130.

These are nice calculations; unfortunately, mathematical facts cannot be questioned.

Having so described the sun, section 134 opens with this remarkable question :

"*Is the sun inhabited ?*"

One feels compelled to look twice at these words; can it be possible the question remains unanswered? Is there room to hope that he will be able to rescue it from the intolerable condition in which he has placed it? Can such a place be the home of men or beasts? We will see.

"If the whole body of the sun is an incandescent globe, of course no organized beings of whom we can conceive can live upon it. But if the incandescence is confined to its photosphere, as many think, and the surface of the globe itself is protected from its outer envelope by a dense atmosphere which absorbs its intense heat and is at the same time a non-conductor of heat, there is nothing to prevent it from being inhabited."—*Elements of Astronomy,* sec. 134.

The state of things described in the section quoted can exist nowhere except when all the physical laws known to us are turned upside down. How can a non-conductor of heat absorb heat? But comment is unnecessary. The section is stamped all over with notice of the fact that it is an ineffectual attempt to avoid the force of our own philosophy.

In section 135 of the same work we read:

"Will the sun keep up forever a supply of the force that has been described? It cannot if it be not replenished, any more than a fire can be kept in unless we put on fuel; any more than a man can work without food. At present philosophers know not by what means it is replenished. As probably there was a time when the sun existed as matter diffused through infinite space, the condensation of which has stored up its heat, so probably there will come a time

when the sun with all the planets welded into its mass will
roll a cold, black ball through infinite space.''

Here, then, is the conclusion of the whole matter.
The infinite universe, according to the professor's
philosophy, began in a whirlwind of fire and is to
end in a coal-black, lifeless mass. When this shall
have taken place, we ask, what will have become of
*indestructible force?* And why should a solar corpse
roll? What benefit or pleasure will its movements
be to him who furnishes the power?

*Such philosophy* has nothing to recommend it. If
it accorded with every known physical principle the
very intuition of a man would rise up and deny it.

In my endeavors to learn what the photosphere of
the sun is, I came across the following from the pen
of Richard A. Proctor:

"Sir William Herschel, in 1777, began a series of solar
observations which before long confirmed Wilson's theory.
He was led to explain the sun's spots by the theory that the
sun's globe is surrounded by two layers of clouds suspended
in an atmosphere at different elevations. He supposed the
upper cloud stratum to be self-luminous, and to be the source
of light or the true photosphere (to use a convenient term
invented by Schrœter). The lower layer he regarded as
opaque, and as owing whatever light it appears to possess to
the reflection of light received from the upper layer. He
supposed that when an opening is formed in the outer layer

we see merely a penumbral spot, but that when the under layer is displaced we see the true surface of the sun, which he supposed to be solid, and not necessarily so heated as to be unfit for habitation. Modern researches show this part at least of Herschel's theory to be wholly untenable, everything tending to prove that the whole mass of the sun to its innermost core is intensely heated."—*American Cyclopædia*, vol. xv., p. 472.

Sir William Herschel was one of the greatest astronomers the world has ever had. His theory so briefly stated lacks nothing except the fact that no example of a self-luminous cloud can be found, and that it furnishes no explanation of the force that is constantly radiating from the sun, and yet it is a more philosophical hypothesis than that of combustion or meteoric collision. However, as we have seen, Proctor pronounces it "*wholly untenable.*" Proceeding further in the article quoted from we read:

"Newton and Buffon conjectured that comets might be the aliment of the sun, and of late years a somewhat similar theory (first broached by Waterson in 1853) has been in vogue, that a stream of meteoric matter constantly pouring into the sun from the regions of space supplies its heat by the conversion of arrested motion. As the sun may indeed derive a small amount of heat from this cause, it deserves more attention than previous conjectures; but conjecture and hypothesis may be said to have given place to views which claim a higher title, as it is now becoming generally recognized in accordance with modern physical theories, that in the gravitation of the sun's mass towards its centre and in its consequent condensation, sufficient heat must be developed to supply the present radiation, enormous as this undoubtedly is. It appears to be susceptible of full demonstration that a *contraction of the sun's volume* of a given definite amount which is yet so slight as to be invisible to the most powerful telescopes *is competent to furnish a heat supply* equal to all that can be emitted during historical periods."— *American Cyclopædia*, vol. xv. p. 476.

If modern researches have as good as proved that the sun is "*intensely heated to its innermost core,*" we want to know who made these researches, and examine their report and learn from it whether the fact is established, or whether they have simply assumed it in order to avoid difficulties which stood in their way.

Of course, a body of matter heated to its centre will take longer to cool than one that is only heated on its surface. So will a large body require more time to cool than a small one. Of course any hot body will become smaller during the time it is cooling; such philosophical principles are susceptible of full demonstration, but they furnish no solution of the solar enigma.

Let the subject under consideration be stated : first, *Is the sun intensely heated?* second, *Is it radiating heat throughout the solar system?* third, *From whence does it obtain a supply?*

Assuming that the first two questions are answered affirmatively. Surely the third cannot be answered by alleging that its "*contraction is competent to furnish the supply.*"

If the sun and planets were at one time glowing with intense heat, we may infer that all the heavenly bodies were at an earlier period in the same condition. What has become of all this heat? When heat was held to be one of the "imponderable substances," we had only to maintain that space is vacant and that the imponderable substances are constantly wasting or escaping into it. But vibration cannot escape into or occupy a vacuum. A vacuum is nothing and therefore not in accord with our best conceptions of unity and infinity. The idea that because something exists, nothing exists *is false.* Sound reasoning leads to the conclusion that in infinite space there can be no empty places. That a sample of every kind of material is around and about us; that the primary forces are also at hand and subject to our examination; that we are in some way their counterpart, both in our physical and in our mental organizations.

Interstellar space, though not a vacuum, is undoubtedly the nearest approach to that imaginary condition. Therefore it is safe to say, that vibrations never escape into it, except when plenty of material is accompanying them.

If all the heavenly bodies have been radiating heat into space for millions of ages, what is the matter with space that it does not get warmed up? When the sun and planets shall be welded into one mass, and *"roll as a cold black ball,"* will not the space occupied by the system be nearer a vacuum than it is now? Is force seeking the vacant places of the universe in which to exhibit its phenomena?

Some years ago I asked a philosopher these questions; he answered, "I am of the opinion that the nebular hypothesis is true, that the planets were at one time white hot, and that they have been cooling down ever since. I believe the vibrations we recognize as heat are all the time wasting into space, or at least are passing out into the tenuous matter lying between the worlds."

"Do you believe," I said, "that light is also a sensation derived from the vibrations of matter?"

"I certainly do," he replied.

"Then," said I, "do you maintain that the light shed abroad by the earth when it was white hot, wasted into space?"

He remarked somewhat brusquely, "I am now

trying to ascertain from what source the sun obtains its supply of heat."

And I replied, " I am trying to find out where its heat has gone to ; when you and I get through, perhaps we had better compare notes."

That same night I inquired of Flex ; answering me he said :

" Scientifically speaking, all that enables us to recognize the existence of material is vibration.   It is that which keeps its elemental particles joined together.   There is no difference between solid, aqueous and gaseous matter, except that due to present and past vibrations.   Wherever in the universe you find matter aggregating you will find the forces accompanying it, and passing on toward the centre of the bodies so formed.   Wherever you find matter expanding, you will find the forces expanding, *i.e.*, proceeding outward with it; this must be the case because the forces are the proximate cause of the fact in either case.   The earth has always been undergoing aggregation and centralization ; therefore its vibrations are now and always have been tending toward its centre.   The earth is hotter now than it ever was, simply because it is larger now than it ever was.   Owing to the aggregation of the earth and sun their interior parts have become hotter and hotter, while the atmosphere lying between them has become thinner and thinner, and therefore colder and colder. This has made our atmosphere shallower (to use an every-day expression), than it was during the geological periods. Therefore the climate of the earth was warmer then than now.

" As to the igneous rocks, lava, etc., you will find no cause for embarrassment. The volcanos of the earth are still adding to the quantity of these on hand. When the continental ranges reared their heads above an universal ocean, there was enough of that kind of material thrown up to satisfy the minds of the most exacting without suggesting the probability that there has been a succession of such upheavals."

We know that our mountain tops even at the equator are perpetually frost covered, and that our polar regions are inaccessible on account of cold, and yet we are asked to believe that the sun has been radiating heat in all directions for millions of ages.

If the power of the sun is only sufficient to warm the central part of the earth's surface and that less than four miles high at the equator, what must be the condition of Mars, to say nothing of Jupiter, Saturn and Uranus? Shall we maintain that the solar system came by chance, and that the earth happened to be in the only habitable location? Can human egotism go further than to suggest that the earth and perhaps a couple of small planets near to it are the only worlds in the solar system in which men can dwell?

Imagine a white hot globe of iron or steel twelve inches in diameter. Let a small frost-covered shot be placed one hundred and twelve feet from it. Now let both globes be rotating on axes nearly parallel to each other. Is it possible to think that the polar extremities of the shot will remain frost covered, and that small elevations on its central parts will remain in the same condition while small depressions around the latter will daily rise to a temperature of one hundred and ten degrees or more?

Now let another shot be placed one hundred and fifty feet from the heated globe; is it not certain that this one will remain frost-covered until every trace of frost is gone from the poles of the other?

If the sun is radiating light throughout the solar system, why is the space between us and the planet Mars dark? Do you ask whether there be any proof that it is dark? Certainly there is. We know that if universal space were lighted up neither the planets or fixed stars would be visible. We also know that in such case philosophers would not be estimating the depth of our atmosphere from calculations based on the duration of twilight..¹ There has never been a better reason given for the color of the sky, than that it is the effect of mingled light and darkness; even Gœthe's idea of white light seen through "turbid media" is not antagonistic to the reason so given.

Does the heat from the sun pass through an immense cold region and make no sign until it reaches the earth, or does it diminish from the time it leaves the sun until it reaches us? We are told that it diminishes in intensity with the square of the distance, but is it force, or is it the sensate phenomenon? If it is the latter, why do we find it colder as we ascend? The man up in a balloon at mid-day has started toward the sun, now since he finds it colder as he rises, will not a radical change have to take place before he reaches a heated body? When will he receive the first premonition that there is a great conflagration directly on his route? Will it be at the first thousand miles, or at the second, or will he reach the sun and then be scorched to death in an instant?

*Then how does the sun light and warm the earth?* An answer to this question cannot be obtained by either experiment or investigation. If answered at all it must be by theory supported by familiar phenomena. Theory is one thing, wild speculation is another thing; when we undertake to plume our imaginations and sail into infinite space we should be supported by the very soundest analogies, otherwise we will be guilty of presumptuous sin.

In Manitou, Colorado, there are several fine mineral springs; near the bottom of one of them about eight or ten feet from its surface, a small glass matrass hangs submerged. Within the matrass there is a loop of very fine wire, its ends so arranged that they can be connected with larger wires leading to an electro-dynamo. The wires form a circuit in which the loop is a connecting link; now when the dynamo is in motion there is a force developed which fills the whole circuit; the larger wires carry it so easily that there is no apparent phenomena, but when it reaches the fine wire it is impeded in its course and the spring is lighted by the incandescence of the loop. This light is nothing more than the phenomenal result of impeded force.

Of course there are no wires connecting the earth and the sun, but the earth's atmospheric molecules arranged pole to pole and equator to equator meet those of the sun arranged in the same manner, and in this contact attraction and repulsion neutralize each other, *i.e.*, establish an equilibrium by means of the rapid changes of magnetic presentation constantly taking place in the molecules. And the force so eliminated must go to the earth and sun, for their movements are producing it.*

We know but little about the atmosphere and less about its molecules; but we may infer that the molecules near the earth and sun are smaller than those farther away from them. It is our immediate molecules that represent the fine wire of the loop; those farther off represent the larger wires leading to the dynamo. The former respond to an overcharge, with transparency and luminous vibration; the latter are filled with the same force but make no sign.

If we were inclined to indulge in mere speculation we would suggest that the molecules are in the form of one of the regular solids,† and such a one as will fill any given space without interstitial loss of room. And that a man may inhale more than a million of them in the valleys of the earth. Perhaps half that number on the tops of the highest mountains. At a height of 100,000 miles his lungs might not be able to take in more than a single specimen, and that might be vibrating so slowly that the lowness of its temperature could not be ascertained or even conjectured. When philosophical analogies are better clas-

---

* See frontispiece, solar and earthly dynamo.

† Since writing the above, the writer has changed his opinion as to the shape of the molecules.

sified and compiled, we think more of them will be
found supporting this speculation than that of the
solar photosphere.

But the atmosphere is said to be a non-conductor
of electricity?

The atmosphere is comparatively a non-conductor,
because it is all the time, both day and night, fully
charged. Therefore, its molecules can receive no
more. The light of the sun and the light of a candle
are each the effect of an overcharge. The incandescent light is the effect of an overcharge at the loop.
The arc light is the effect of the overcharged atmosphere between the carbons.

How does a burning candle develop electricity *alias*
magnetic force? By the rapid decomposition of fat
which was once an overcharge in the animal, *an
overcharge of force.* Combustion is setting this force
free, and the molecules are returning it to the earth
from whence it came.

Combustion is one of the most abstruse subjects in
philosophy. We will not attempt to explain it.
But we will say that the circuits of force proceeding
from a burning candle are in some respects directly
opposite in character to those that proceed from the
earth and sun, for the latter are not at present undergoing decomposition but the reverse.

The incandescent light is an example of force passing through darkness and cold and becoming light and
heat at the place where it is impeded. The propul-
sion of street cars by electricity furnishes an example
of the transmission of the same force without impedition. Such every-day examples of the peculiarities
of force ought to have some effect on our general
philosophy.

One more example. Some years ago Dr. John W.
Draper made a series of experiments with lenses. In
one of these experiments he arranged a twelve-inch
lens so that the cone of rays proceeding from the sun
met in the centre of a glass matrass, six inches in
diameter, filled with water.

This eminent experimenter observed that the water
became warm at the focus. Indeed, he saw the hot
water ascending from the focus. In this example
the force passed through the glass and three inches
into the water without making any sign except a
slight change of direction, but when the converging
rays met at the focal point, they impeded the course
of each other and the force changed to heat. Heat
is a sluggish phenomenon; force is swifter than the
lightning's flash. Had it been heat radiating from
the sun, the water would have absorbed it, *i.e.*, received its vibrations long before they reached the

focus. Indeed, the atmosphere would have received them before they reached the matrass. If any one has ever been able to focus the rays of heat proceeding from fire, he has not announced the fact.

Place two magnets on a table so that they will attract each other, but not so near that the force will bring them together. Reflect upon their condition as they lie there straining at each other. There is no movement; yet there is a force acting between them. Magnetic life has come within reach of its affinity, and the two magnets would instantly become one magnet if they were in suspension. Reflect again. Possibly the molecules of the atmosphere in their immediate neighborhood have arranged themselves in conformity to the forceful currents so established, but we cannot prove it. The only thing we do know is that force is at work and that it is resisted, and we may infer that if the magnets were great enough, the power that seeks to bring them together, acting against the power that keeps them apart would manifest itself in light and heat. That such would be the result is not a speculation of ours; it is one of the certainties of science.

Now call to your mind the fact that our ablest astronomers and physicists are thoroughly convinced that this same forceful connection exists between the earth and the sun. Is there any room to hesitate? Is it not certain that the result is light and heat? That we are not able to discover either light or heat in our petty example signifies nothing. Some of the most important things in the universe cannot be seen and some of them cannot be recognized by any of our senses. Force is one of these when considered apart from sensate phenomena. If we are to believe nothing except that which we can see and understand, we may as well dismiss all philosophical inquiry from our minds, for in such case the solar enigma is not worth solving.

Suppose we cannot explain the manner in which force changes to light or heat, is there any one who doubts it? Admit that force is also a phenomenon. Are material things more real than that which moves them from place to place? Are the earth and sun more real than the power that sustains them in their orbits?

The sun is a glorious body. Years ago I hoped hereafter to make my home in it. I imagined that some time I would stroll through its green fields, climb its mighty mountains and navigate its rivers and oceans. I have not the shadow of a doubt that it is inhabited. Therefore, I strenuously object to its people being smothered under a philosophical photosphere or " hot potted " in a Dutch oven.

*Is the sun an incandescent body of matter?* *From whence does it obtain a supply of heat?* We will answer the first question in the negative, and offer the following as a solution of the solar enigma.

Consider the universe as one body of matter in which many aggregations have taken place because of the inherent attractive and repellant forces existing in every particle of matter. Consider that the earth exists because of its own cohesiveness exerted against every other body of matter in the universe, and particularly against the sun, with which it is more intimately connected. Then mutual attraction, repulsion and adjustment becomes the primary scientific cause of all natural phenomena.

*From whence came this inherent force?* There can be no answer, except that given by the reflex, " *From God Almighty.*"

# CHAPTER VI.

## SNOW CRYSTALS.

ONE Saturday night I sat in the library reading "Ragnarok, or the Age of Fire and Gravel." Presently the clock struck ten, then closing the book I began to think about the earth, how curiously it had been formed of primordial matter, and wondering what kind of material the latter was, and whether magnetic force really did gather it and shape it into a great round world. If this be so, I thought, then it must have piled the materials around the magnetic lines that exist in the earth and around the earth. I will examine this subject by the way of analogy.

There was a plate of apples on the table. Taking the finest one, I held it up by the stem and said, "You shall represent the earth, a molecule of air, or anything that is a magnet. Your stem shall be your north pole, your blossom end your south pole, and I will carve you on the dynamic lines;" I then inserted the point of a knife at its north magnetic parallel slanting towards its centre. Then pressing the knife to the core, and cutting around in the direction indi-

cated I severed a conic section and laid it on the table.
I then took a similar section from the blossom end
and laid that also aside; the remaining section re-
sembled a double concave lens, but the slope of the
cut was too angular for that, so I hardly knew what
to call it.  However, I held it up and tried to look
through the centre of it, but though the light pene-
trated it I could not see through it, yet I peered into
it as inquisitively as if I had expected the core to
yield results of an astonishing character.  Still holding it in my hand I thought; "Suppose this section
really were a section taken from some great planet
like the earth?  How easy it would be for a person
on one side of it to hear suggestions from the other
side.  In such case he would not know from whence
they came.  And he might not be able to convince
anybody that he heard anything.  It looks like a
*whispering place.*  When I have more leisure I will
inquire into it."

Then I reconstructed the apple and cut it in half
from the stem to blossom end.  Looking at the cut
surface of one of the halves, I studied the dynamic
lines and I also made a diagram of them for present
use and future reference, Fig. 16.

"This," I said, looking at the diagram ; "Is the
magnetic frame; the very dynamic skeleton on which

the earth was formed. Around these lines the material clustered until it became a world." As I studied the diagram I seemed to have a faint remembrance of a thousand things resembling it. *Six points!* I said, "What is it that seems so familiar to me? Somewhere I have seen six pointed stars in great numbers and if I am not mistaken they were direct from nature's workshop; *fresh minted; —* *Where could it have been?*"

FIG. 16.

Reflecting in this way, it presently came to my mind that they were snow crystals. Then opening Steele's *Fourteen Weeks' in Philosophy*, at p. 253, I found a picture of sixteen very fine specimens with the comments of the author on their wonderful beauty and variety,* Fig. 17. I noticed that notwithstanding their great variety, they were all constructed on the same general plan. Six points projecting from a

---

* In Warren's *New Physical Geography*, there is a cut containing thirty-two specimens, all of which are hexagons. In this work it is stated that they may be seen on a "dark cloth with the aid of a microscope." I have seen them on the ground without such aid ; I never saw any that were not hexagons.

hexagonal frame; however, three of them vary
slightly from the plan. One of them has twelve
points, which is a multiple of six; another is an open
triangle, the lines of which being double I had only
to imagine them separated and then it also conformed
to the general plan. The third is a small cylinder
with three hexagonal buttons strung on it at equal

Fig. 17.

distances from each other. It also is a handsome
specimen and yet it seems out of place among its su-
periors. I concluded that it was intended to emphasize the fact that there is no rule in nature or art
that is not subject to exceptions.

Still considering the subject, I thought, why should

these crystals bear the image of the earth's forces? Why should not some of them have five points, or seven, or any number of points? What has caused them to conform so nearly to a general plan? These may be simple questions, I thought, but they are not easily answered.

Looking again at the crystals and the diagram, and thinking about the forces represented by them and the amazing work of world formation, it occurred to me that the atmosphere is probably a residue of primordial matter and that drops of water in suspension are probably minature worlds. Accepting this to be the truth, I concluded, that as the tiny trembling drops congealed, it was magnetic force that departed from them, leaving a delicate tracery of ice in the very image of its three circuits, Fig. 18.

Then I noticed that Flex had come in and was standing by examining the crystals and the diagram, and I said: "Is there any error in this line of thought?"

"Not as far as you have gone," he replied, "but there is an important matter which you have not taken into consideration. Look again at the crystals and you will see that nearly all of them have a central piece in which the hexagon is again exhibited. Now draw your diagram so that it will show the

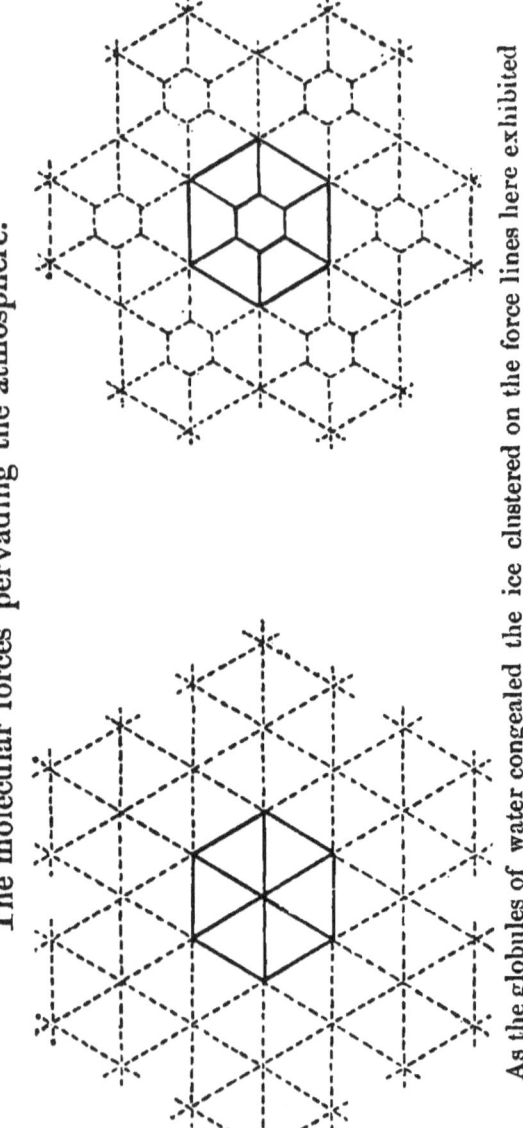

Fig. 18.

The molecular forces pervading the atmosphere.

As the globules of water congealed the ice clustered on the force lines here exhibited forming the crystals. Disturbances caused by sound will account for much of their beauty and variety.

course of the first and second circuits (Fig. 19).
You will observe that they repel each other near the
centre of the diagram. The effect of this is the most
important subject in science. From it arises the
third circuit; the central piece in the crystals is the
junctional effect of the forces at that place. As some
of the crystals do not exhibit its effects you may be
sure that some counterforce has been at work. There
is a lesson in this which I leave to your own reflection.

"Heat and cold are among the first expressions
of primary force. We
know that they are vi-
brations of the atmos-
phere or of an universal
ether. The former we
know something about,
the latter is only a sup-

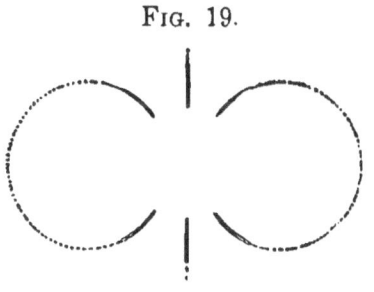

Fig. 19.

position and like the solar photosphere (invented by
Schrœter), its existence may be more than doubted.

"The atmosphere is composed of minute particles
of matter; we assume them to be endowed with magnetism. Light and darkness being vibrations of these
particles, the latter should in some way exhibit the
impress of the forces involved in their existence.
Place your pencil at the north pole of the diagram,

Fig. 20.   Look sharp now! The color is there.
The south pole answers, the north pole being in the
same circuit and the color is violet.   Bring your pencil down to the north magnetic parallel; the south
magnetic parallel responds and the color is blue;
now touch the third circuit and you have the first
life color, that of vegetation, green.   Carry your
pencil to the south magnetic parallel and again the
north magnetic parallel answers, and the color is
yellow; to the south
pole and we have in-
digo; back to the south
magnetic parallel, or-
ange.   Now touch the
whispering place and
you have the second
life color, that of ani-
mals, red.   The forces involved can make no other
changes of movement.

FIG. 20.

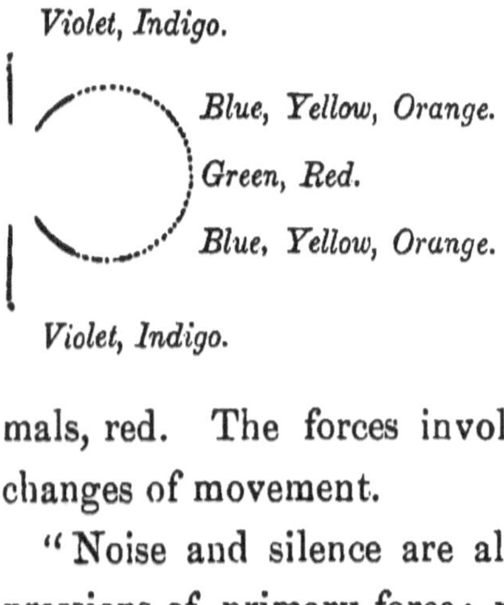

Violet, Indigo.

Blue, Yellow, Orange.

Green, Red.

Blue, Yellow, Orange.

Violet, Indigo.

"Noise and silence are also among the first expressions of primary force; place your pencil again
at the north pole, Fig. 21.   Sound it, and you will
hear a full tone sweep from north to south through
the first circuit.   Bring your pencil down to the north
magnetic parallel; the second circuit responds
throughout with its first full tone.   Now touch the

third circuit and note the sweetness of the semitone.
To the south magnetic parallel for the second full
tone of the second circuit.   Now to the south pole for
the second full tone of the first circuit; return to the
south magnetic parallel for the third full tone of the
second circuit; now touch the third circuit, and
again you have the semitone and the sound dies at
the whispering place.   *Seven points !*   The forces of
the universe have responded to the
force you have applied to its constituents.   And since you were careful the effect has been harmonious.
This is the ' music of the spheres.'
It was the morning stars that sang
together when the earth started on
its first orbital revolution.

FIG. 21.

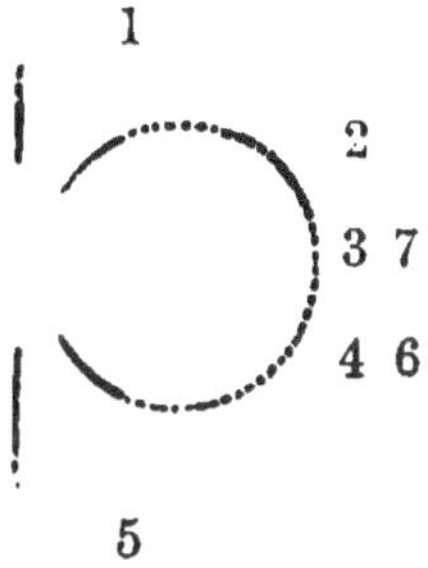

"Do you want a more tangible illustration?  strike
a bar of steel with a hammer; note the vibrations as
they proceed from both ends to the centre, then again
to the ends and back to the centre, Fig. 22.  This
comprises all the different movements the bar can
make.  No matter how long it continues to vibrate,
it comes to rest at its centre; its lingering last throb
is the seventh point.

"This is somewhat the manner in which the watery
globules vibrated in the example of heat and cold;

the centre piece of the crystals was the last expression of force. So the atmospheric molecules vibrated in the example of light and darkness—and red was their last expression. So in sound the semitone finishes the scale.

"To be more explicit, there are three circuits; 1, 2, 3. These numbers are subject to six permutations, and as they represent force, equilibrium is the seventh expresssion.

"Although our last example fairly illustrates the permutation of the forces, it is misleading in other respects. The bar is comparatively free at both ends, the atmospheric molecules are not, but are connected with each other by their first circuits of attractive force. When force is applied to the molecules it proceeds in polar directions until it is lost in the infinity of the first circuit; it also proceeds curvilineally outwardly until it is lost in the junction of the second and first circuits. From which you will understand that the molecules when considered as forceful lines are fast at both ends. Of course, they drift hither and thither; so may a magnetic needle be carried from place to place ; yet both the needle and the molecules

FIG. 22.

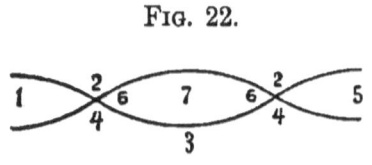

are endeavoring to obey the forces within them, and these are continually contending with the forces around and about them. The earth and all the heavenly bodies are in the same condition; they are all trembling under the power of the infinite conflicting forces; they may never reach an equilibrial adjustment.

"The string of a musical instrument being fast at both ends is compelled to vibrate in precisely the same manner that the molecules vibrate. Therefore, a thrummed string strikes nature's forces in perfect accord. For this reason, stringed instruments send forth the sweetest sounds that primary force can produce." Flex paused for a moment and I ventured to ask, "what is the shape of an atmospheric molecule?"

"Molecules," he replied, "are simply little masses of matter more or less endowed with magnetic force. Atmospheric molecules are little masses of gaseous matter so endowed; if it is one of these you have in mind, your question can be answered, but the answer may not be very satisfactory. On the other hand, if you have in contemplation an 'atom,' or some ultimate division of matter, I can only remind you that the universe itself is the only ultimate atom.

"Every true philosophical concept has its counter-

part in nature. The universe does not consist of an
infinite series of causes and effects leading up to an
ultimatum or down to an ultimatum. The idea that
such is the case is in parity with the idea that there
can be a highest and a lowest degree of temperature,
the smallest fraction and the greatest whole number.
The best conception of the universe is that which regards everything in nature as being at the same time
both cause and effect ; vibration as the cause of temperature and temperature the cause of vibration.
This is absolutely true as to all the primary forces
and relatively true as to every permutation of them.

"The best philosophical conception of God is that
which regards Him as the life of the universe. The
infinite, bodily, mental, and spiritual entirety. That
which is infinite in unity must be infinite in divis-
ibility ; therefore, an ' *ultimate atom* ' is an unphilo-
sophical conception and cannot exist.

"Our philosophy is unsatisfactory mainly because
we refuse to accept the infinite in every branch of
science except in mathematics and astronomy. We
do not comprehend it in either of the branches mentioned : we simply accept it as a true philosophical
conception.

"In physics we cannot comprehend a body of
matter moving in opposite directions at the same time.

Yet, we can comprehend a body of matter vibrating in opposite directions at the rate of a thousand times a minute. And we can and do conceive that there are vibrations of matter involved in the production of light exceeding five hundred trillions a second.* We can as readily conceive them at the rate of a hundred thousand decillions a second. Admitting this, vibrations of infinite rapidity become a true philosophical conception, and the counterpart of this conception would be a body of matter moving in both directions at the same time. This is a conception of infinite rectilineal motion. I make these remarks because your question leads us slightly into the domain of infinite dexterity.

" Force exists in three primary expressions : attraction, repulsion, and equilibrium. Matter exists in three primary shapes : the spherical, the spheroidal and the geometrical. Motion exists in three primary forms : the rectilineal, the elliptical, and the circular.

"Magnetism furnishes an example of attraction and repulsion ; the air an example of universal equilibrium, inasmuch as it will not allow any portion of the universe to be emptied. Globules of water in

---

* Fraunhofer estimates the rapidity of light-vibrations as follows : For the middle violet, 733,000,000,000,000 per second ; for the middle red, 500,000,000,000,000,

suspension are examples of the sphere; the earth and heavenly bodies are examples of the spheroidal shape. Earthy crystals, salt, alum, sulphur, etc., are examples of the geometrical shape.

"The rotation of the earth on its axis is an example of circular motion; its orbital revolution an example of elliptical motion.

"Now where is there an example in nature of rectilineal motion ?

"Rectilineal motion is a true philosophical conception and therefore it exists somewhere in the universe. *Where ?*

"There are no secrets in nature, no expression of force which we cannot experiment with; no kind of matter except such as we have samples of, and no phenomena except such as are exhibited to us freely. We are not the victims of either fraud or deception. Broad daylight and fair play prevails here and elsewhere throughout the universe. Yet there are an infinite number of simple things which neither you or I understand, mainly because we refuse to accept the absolute, and demand reasons for things which are in their very nature self-evident.

"Comparative rest and uniform temperature at a certain degree transform the simple and almost homogeneous substance of an egg into a chick. We may learn how this takes place, but a comprehension of it is beyond our present attainments.

"Scientifically considered, the force of attraction demands all material to aggregate into one central, motionless, 'cold black ball;' universal equilibrium compels it to accept an infinite number of aggregations, hence the chief characteristics of the larger aggregations are rigidity, a spheroidal shape, rotation and exterior changes of magnetic presentation.

"Repellant force alone would separate all material into one homogeneous entirety. Equilibrium compels it to accept an infinite number of gaseous molecules in such a condition as enables them to keep all space filled regardless of past, present, and future aggregation, hence the chief characteristics of gaseous molecules are elasticity, an accommodating shape, rapid internal changes of magnetic presentation and dexterity.

Fig. 23.

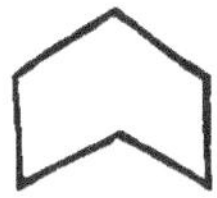

Molecule, general outline.

"The shape of an atmospheric molecule, if one could be seen at rest, is nearly that of a short bee-cell, Fig. 23. It may be described as a hexagonal cylinder terminating in an extended hexagonal frustum at one end, and a sunken impression of the same frustum at the other. They are of course, always in mass, and when masses of them are comparatively at rest they are telescoped into each other in long files, so arranged that the

Fig. 24.

north pole of every molecule in file is internally approaching the north pole of the molecule next north. We will call this position *north check*, Fig. 24. This is a *like presentation and therefore a repellant one.* The elasticity of the molecules enables them to respond, and the whole file immediately springs back in a right line to a reverse position, in which position all their south poles are presented to each other and again they execute the same movement. We will call the second position *south check*, Fig. 25.

North Check.

Fig. 25.

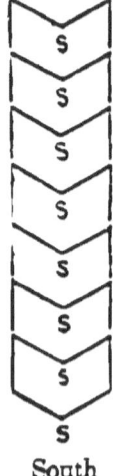

South Check.

"When a file of molecules are at north check, there is an instantaneous spurt of material and force angularly outward toward the south molecular hinges or joints. When they are at south check this action is reversed, Fig. 26. As the reversals take place with inconceivable rapidity both actions may be regarded as taking place at the same moment. If the files could be seen so rapidly vibrating north and south, they would appear as a combination of both movements, Fig. 27.

" The force so evolved cannot be received by the impinging files for they are in the same state. Hence each molecule is compelled to expand from its centre to its equatorial circumference and shrink from the latter to its centre in alternate correspondence to its polar action.

" This gives to the molecules intermediately between north and south check a more curvilineal appearance, and also causes a slight separation of them in file, Fig. 28.

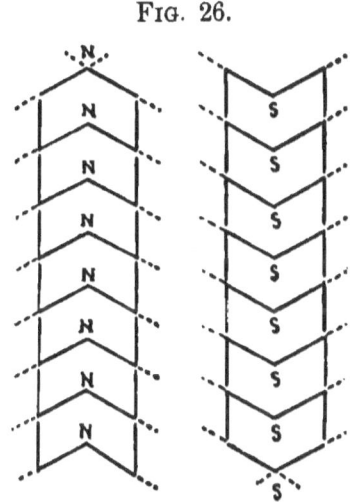

FIG. 26.

Instantaneous emissions of force and matter when the reversals take place.

" Now as the position of the molecules is horizontal at the equator, and as they are in mass, their lateral vibrations strike the earth with rapid *vertical pulsations at the equator* and in a more angular manner as the latitude increases north or south. We recognize these pulsations in the atmosphere as light, and heat is evolved by the resistance they meet with at the surface of the earth. The intensity of solar heat depends entirely on the directness or indirectness of the molecular stroke. On a hot summer day near the equator these pulsations can be felt.

"You will understand from the premises that the third circuit of magnetic force springs from a combination or rather a contest of the first and second circuits and that it manifests itself to us in natural phenomena.

FIG. 27.

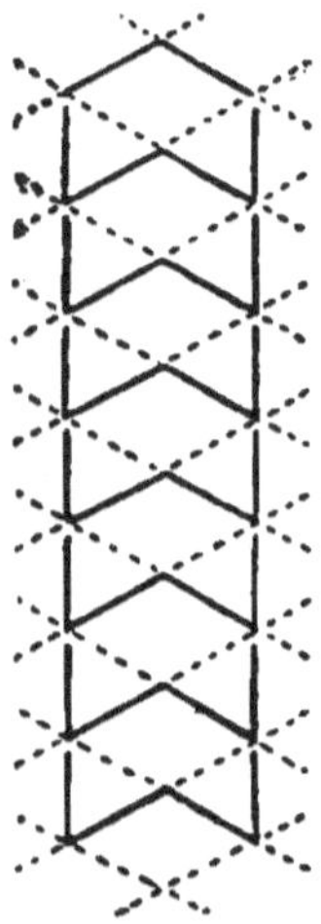

Short file of molecules, internal view. Rapid vibration.

"Molecular vibrations (even when no light is produced) may be safely stated to be at the rate of one hundred trillion reversals a second. This is practically a continuous current of rectilineal force flowing north and south at the same time. *This is the first circuit of magnetic force.*

"There is also at the same time a continuous current of force springing outwardly and inwardly at the molecular joints; (and of course a similar current at the magnetic poles of the earth?) *This is the second circuit.* The spherical expansion and contraction arising from the forces referred to *is the third circuit.*

"It is as you will realize the inconceivable rapidity of magnetic reversal that leads the telegraph operator to suppose that his messages pass to and fro at the same instant. Practically they do; scientifically they pass in one direction during one impulse, and in the other direction during the reversed impulse, though the word *during* hardly applies to pulsations which occur in the one hundred trillionth part of a second. If we could see the molecules in mass as they appear in the atmosphere we would notice great masses of files drifting hither and thither. In some places coiling up and in other places unfolding, and at the same time shrinking and expanding longitudinally and laterally like the movements of a caterpillar. Occasionally great numbers of detached ones would be seen skipping about with wonderful celerity and attaching themselves to each other and to other files presenting the appearance of some varieties of coral formation. This appearance is, however, as evanescent as a flash of lightning.*

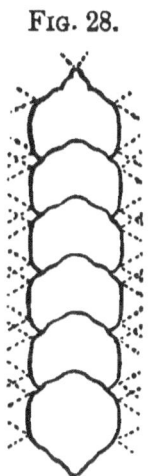

Fɪɢ. 28.

Short file of molecules external view. Slower vibration.

" During a thunder storm we would notice that the contraction of the files was increasing and the

---

* When the air is disturbed by the voice of a fine singer its molecules frequently assume the form of plants, trees and flowers.

7

molecules *telescoping more closely into each other,* some of them apparently swallowing whole files. Closely observing these we would perceive that they became larger and of firmer material and that this enabled them to usurp more room, and at the same time assume a more spherical shape, and presently we would see great numbers of them falling as drops of water, some of which would reach the earth while others would be absorbed by the files through which they descended.

"Again if we could see a single molecule in perspective, rapidly undergoing the transposition of its polar extremities its shape would be that of a hexagonal solid with eighteen facets. Of these six hexagons form the equatorial belt. Twelve quadrangles, with their sharp angles focused at the poles and their broad ends fitting into the equatorial facets complete the figure.

FIG. 29.

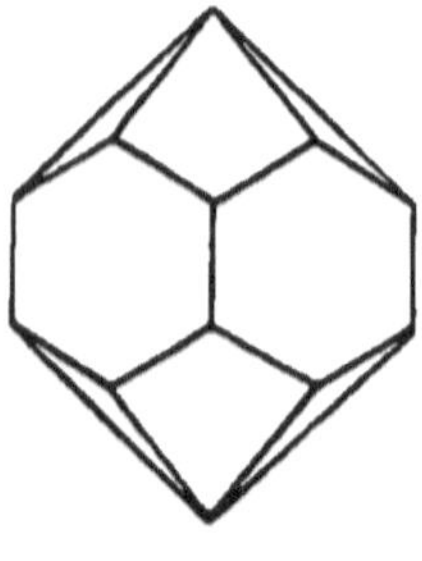

"To construct this figure; plane a stick of wood until it has six equal sides, saw off a block in length equal to the greater diameter of the stick, then bevel the ends down at the corners to a point, preserving the hexagon facets all round the centre of the block.

" So constructed the figure has twenty-six exterior angles, namely, two polar angles, and six upper, and six lower junctional angles located north and the same number south of its equator, Fig. 29.

" The molecules themselves in mass have only twelve exterior angles and two interior angles. The others are the effect of inconceivable rapid vibration. *It is not matter we are considering but force.* Now since the atmosphere is the basis of all sound, we conclude that the twenty-six sounds represented by the English alphabet comprise every articulate sound the human voice can make, and that some of them are merely lingual luxuries. Again, calling your attention to the shape of the molecules when *at check*, we observe that it is only a little too much angularity that prevents them from being in the shape of a heart, and that their action is that of a great number of hearts acting in unison, Fig. 30. And at the same time we realize that each one of them is a separate individuality pulsating throughout its entire body, and sending both matter and force toward the molecular extremities and joints.

FIG. 30.

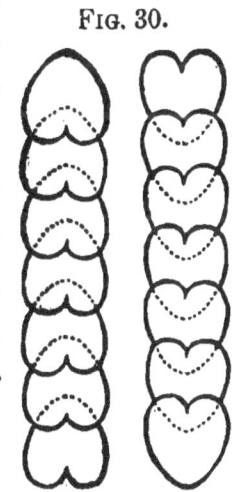

Curvilineal view of molecules in file.

"Accepting these analogies for what they seem to be worth, we have three primary expressions of force—attraction, repulsion, and equilibrium. Three primary kinds of matter—atmospheric, aqueous, and solid. Three primary forms of motion—rectilineal, circular, and elliptical. Three primary kinds of life —molecular, vegetable, and animal.

"Two currents of force can no more occupy the same body of matter at the same time, than can two bodies of matter occupy the same place at the same time, and yet in about one-half of the snow crystals we see the force-lines crossing each other in the centre of the crystals at angles of sixty degrees, Fig. 31. This apparent contradiction of our conclusions arises from the fact that in the crystals we simply see the impress of the forces spread upon a plane, which is not at all the form in which they occupied the globules of water; nor the form in which they occupy the earth.*

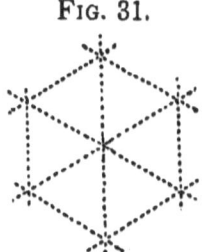

Fig. 31.

* When the earth was a molecule, its "true magnetic poles" (like those of the snow crystals) were located thirty degrees from its equator. That they are now near the sixtieth degrees of north and south latitude is due to the inequality in the size of the earth and sun.

"If we take one of these crystals and cause it to rotate on its centre, we shall have a polar projection of magnetic force, Fig. 32; the same view may also be obtained by looking at the end of a bar-magnet with iron filings attached (see Fig. 6). The centre of the crystal is of course at rest.

FIG. 32.

"About one-half of the crystals exhibit an open centre expanded into hexagons, Fig. 33. If we assume two opposite points of this crystal to be its poles, and then conceive the whole figure rotating on the polar axis we have selected, the figure so produced will be a sphere, Fig. 34, and we realize that the centre of it is at rest, or in equilibrium, and that all the matter composing it is being thrown towards its surface. This ideal figure may also be obtained by conceiving a bar-magnet with iron filings surrounding it, the whole in absolute equilibrium (see Fig. 5).

FIG. 33.

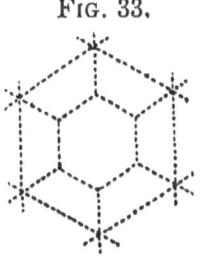

"This peculiar and almost indescribable motion is the effect of all the forces combined. It is in the nature of a curvilineal adjustment of two rectilineal forces acting in different directions in the same body of matter. In short, it is an alternate spherical expansion and contraction within bodies of matter controlled by the magnetic forces on their surface. We recognize it as heat and cold, *i.e.*, temperature.

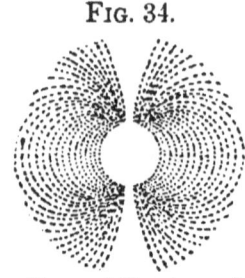

FIG. 34.

Central Section of Sphere in plane.

"Temperature is the first sensate phenomenon. The third expression of force. Its tendency is to exclude all other expressions of force from the interior of all bodies of matter."

Here Flex paused a moment and addressing me more directly said :

"You are becoming too sleepy to understand the facts I am presenting. If you will rouse yourself for a short time, I will explain an interesting theory or rather an hypothesis which may be called, *molecular incubation.* Leaving out all the details it may be briefly stated as follows :

"A globule of water in suspension contains every elemental ingredient found in the earth or around the earth. At the moment it assumes the spherical shape, its centre is at thirty-two degrees of temperature, Fahrenheit. During *this moment* the earthy matter in the globule radiates from its centre toward its circumference as if the laws of gravitation were reversed, and the earthy matter near its surface sinks inwardly as if the globule were a miniature world. The earth at some period of time became an aggregation of these drops of water. As accumulation proceeded the earthy matter in the water radiated outwardly from the centre of the earth and inwardly from its surface; forming an intermediate crust of solid matter surrounding its equatorial zone, and extending towards its magnetic poles. The polar core was filled with water at all times, and served as an escape for the accumulating gases.

"As the earth increased in size its sedimental crust expanded, leaving a large body of water in the interior, the water changing into deep warm mud at the interior surface. From time to time this interior world became more and more separated from every kind of phenomena except darkness, temperature, and perhaps slight magnetic disturbances. The forces of expansion and contraction meeting each other at the centre of the crust caused heat in that locality, and this divided the interior surface of the crust into zones with warm water and mud near the equator, and cooler water and mud near the magnetic poles. But these extremes were very slight.

"Here in the interior of the earth, in darkness, silence, and rest, *molecular life* (or activity which-

ever you please to call it) developed and differentiated into two principal classes of higher life, both
wholly unlike anything on the outside of the earth.

"For convenience we will call these classes *polar*
and *central*.

"The *polar class* were subjected to six months
more or less in which it was quite cool, and during
such times many of them dissipated into air, earth,
and water. The air so disengaged went toward the
polar core and ultimately became free on the outside
of the earth. The earthy matter became part of the
muddy mass, thereby increasing the thickness of the
crust. In time this process of disintegration broke
up the molecular files into fragments consisting of
single molecules, double molecules, and short and
long lengths. During the six months in which it
was cooler, all of these varieties would shrink in at
their polar extremities and become more compact and
globular in their appearance. At such times there
was very little if any perceptible difference between
the varieties referred to. All of them were simply
little hard compact balls with the molecular life
principle lying dormant in the centre. During the
warmer six months they would all open slightly at
their poles and increase slightly in size, and a subtile
essence would exude from their poles and from their

molecular joints. But as the single molecules had no such joints, they would collapse when the cooler period began, and open somewhat in the manner of an oyster when the warmth returned. For untold ages this went on until each of these varieties were nothing but infinitesimal seeds of molecular life. So far as eyes could see an homogeneous mass of black mud. Now leaving this class for the present.

" The *central* class meanwhile differentiated on entirely different lines. They also kept *telescoping into each other* in file, and becoming from century to century more and more expanded. Those in favored localities, such as proximity to the equator and the deeper and warmer places, grew larger than the others, and their valvular action became more expanded and at the same time less rapid. As the files expanded and contracted there was constantly emitted from the molecular joints the same essence emitted by the class first referred to but in much greater quantities. In time, this exudation combined with mineral substances in solution, encrusted the molecular joints. In the various limestone regions this took place fast, causing imperfect valvular action, and a supension of all action throughout many large regions. In such places there were hundreds of cubic miles of imperfect shells left telescoped together.

"So incrustation and want of uniformity in size ultimately broke up the files into singles, doubles, and short and long lengths.

"Molecular action in the longer files tended toward the ends. As the intermediate action became more and more imperfect, both ends became funnel-shaped and still kept on expanding and contracting; after while these would part and form two short files, and then the dead ends of each file would slough off leaving broad terminations.

"Sometimes the short files developed superior and inferior terminations from the start, Fig. 35. Other files seemed unable to determine which should be their principal and which their subsidiary end, consequently they made little or no development at either extremity, but in lieu thereof threw out extensions all along their sides at the molecular joints, and these moved backward and forward in correspondence to a very weak and slow internal palpitation, Fig. 36.

FIG. 35.

Valvular Development.

"Double molecules maintained valvular action at both ends, at the same time opening and closing at their joints. Their action was weak from the start,

and they soon became encrusted at their ends, leaving
them only an opening at
the joint. This action
soon developed a hinge
on the opposite side.
They then threw out
siphon-like extensions and this completed their development.

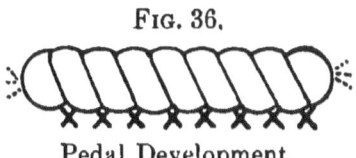

FIG. 36.

Pedal Development.

" Single molecules could at first only palpitate
back and forth in the soft warm mud. Later some
of them attached themselves to the ground by suc-
tion, and as they became encrusted developed holes
in their upper surfaces. Others collapsed, assuming
the general form of double molecules with a back
hinge, but they were not able to project any extensions from the opening so formed.

" About this time the earth which had been all the
while subject to occasional disturbances which could
be felt on both its inner and outer surfaces, opened
near one of its magnetic poles, and there issued a
very large volume of warm water and black mud
containing all the germs of life. The polar class
buried in the low-lands of the earth found conditions
not far removed from what they had been subjected
to, and in the returning spring they expanded slightly
at their poles and the subtile essence of molecular

life took root at one end and sprang upward at the
other, and the warm moist ground nourished the
roots of them and the bright light kissed the tops of
them, and shortly thereafter the earth 'stood dressed
in living green.' The *central class* perished immediately, the principal cause being want of proper
aliment. After this the devolopment of molecular
life inside the earth proceeded as before.

"Many centuries thereafter the earth opened again
and emitted another great flood of life surpassing in
volume and variety anything we can conceive. At
this time the best developed but not the most perfect
organizations of the central class survived and filled
all the waters of the earth with fish. And again, the
polar class took root and grew. And molecular development inside the earth proceeded as before.
Then after ages had elapsed the earth opened the
third time. This time a bountiful supply of all
classes and varieties survived. Yet the earth was
almost covered and the seas almost filled with the
shells and bones of the dead.

"Analogies supporting this theory may be found
in the shape of the flower-buds and fruits of vegetation, particularly in that of seeds and nuts, the ker-
nels of which are almost invariably composed of two
lobes, which is an evidence of their molecular origin.

They may also be found in the animal kingdom beginning with the earliest forms of organized life, the
fossil remains of which are found in
the rocks, Fig. 37. Sometimes clus-
ters of crinoids so closely resemble the
foliage of plants and trees that it is
nearly or quite impossible to determine whether they were a vegetable or
an animal organization. Indeed, there
is no dividing line between vegetable
life and animal life. Neither is there a
dividing line between vegetable life and molecular

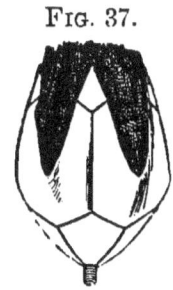

FIG. 37.

Silurian Blas-
toid.*

---

* This species of animal life began its existence in the
upper Silurian and culminated in the Carboniferous age.
When closed as they are in the fossil state they look like
flower-buds, many varieties of which they also resemble in
that they are composed of five petal-like ambulacra. Their
general appearance is much like one of the shapes assumed
by molecules, yet there is a great difference; molecules are
hexagonal, blastoids are pentagonal. This similarity and
want of similarity is another variation of the old puzzle.
When we contemplate mankind as having descended from
some inferior race of animals, the question arises, *what has
become of the tail?* So in contemplating blastoids and flower-
buds as having descended from molecules, the same question
meets us at the threshold, *what has become of the sixth expression of force?*

life. The higher and lower forms invariably blend into each other like the colors of a rainbow.

"Suggestions of molecular aggregation are apparent in all the insects. We can almost count the number of molecules composing them. The sections in their larvæ can be counted. Their eyes, too, are frequently a collection of hexagonal facets, a wonderful exhibition of molecular persistence and adequacy.

"That many insects are but little advanced beyond the molecular condition is manifested by the dexterity of their movements, and also by their comparative exemption from pain. Flies that have lost a leg seem but little if any the worse off, and wasps that have been cut in halves will eat the severed part of their own bodies.

"In the higher animals, departures from original forms are very wide, yet their anatomies and particularly their spines denote a compilation of molecules. The animal heart is a curvilineal fleshy development of the molecule, its action is precisely the same, the vital fluid proceeds from it and returns to it in the same general directions. In short the difference between them, amounts to about this, *the rapid vibration of the molecule has given place to the slow and orderly palpitation of the heart.*

"We are apt to think that all things were instantaneously created by the voice of Omnipotence, but that is not God's way, at least not his way on this earth. It takes several weeks for an egg to hatch. So it requires nine months time in comparative quietness, darkness, and an equable temperature, and then a child is born. These are the works of Omnipotence! *Natural events!* because we see them daily. So it required ages within the bowels of the earth, and then at the appointed times there came forth the handiwork of Omnipotence. We were not present when the earth was delivered, but to those who were it was a *natural event!* which for a long time had been expected.

"Of course all this begins and ends in theory, yet the analogies are sufficient to render it probable that God in the manner indicated, furnished the earth with every incipient form of life. And we may conclude that no creature emitted from the bowels of the earth possessed any sense except that of feeling, yet feeling implies ease and pain, sexual relationship, reproduction, and death.

"Now returning to the main subject which is one of more importance since it leads to an understanding of what is to take place in the future, I will offer you one more example of primary phenomena.

"Our senses being complemental to the movements of primary force, they are of course arranged in the same order."

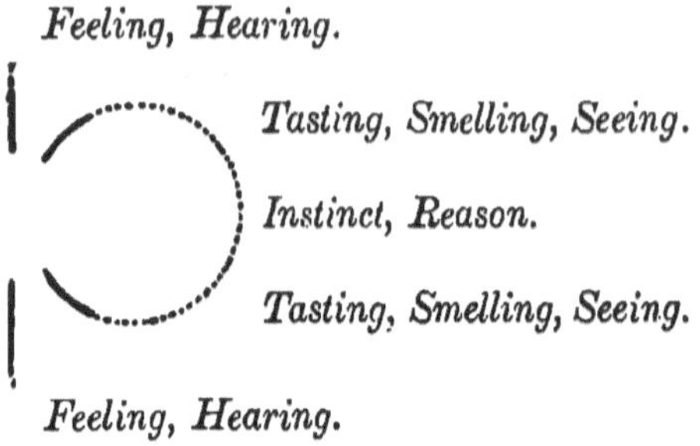

The clock struck twelve. I answered it dreamily, "*seven points !*"

FIG. 38.

*Feeling, Hearing.*

*Tasting, Smelling, Seeing.*

*Instinct, Reason.*

*Tasting, Smelling, Seeing.*

*Feeling, Hearing.*

"It is the Sabbath day," said Flex.

"The forces we have been considering have invariably rested at their seventh expression. Let us recognize the importance of the fact and at the same time obey the commandment of our Creator."

# CHAPTER VII.

## THE BEST EVIDENCE.

LAST Saturday night we undertook an examination of primary force, but owing to human frailty we drifted into snow and out of that into music and color, and some of the very smallest things and then sleep and Sunday morning overcame us and so very little of importance was accomplished.

But to-night we intend to keep awake and notice a few things which have the impress of the forces plainly stamped upon them, and by analogy endeavor to demonstrate the fact that there is more than an accidental correlation between the smallest things and the greatest results.

But before proceeding with the subject I will tell you what I dreamed the night we labored among the crystals. Not that I attach much importance to dreams, but because mine was an odd one, and so far I have not found any person able to interpret it.

It seemed to me that Flex and I were on the summit of Pike's Peak and that he was provided with a very fine telescope with which he was surveying the heavens; I thought it was in the night and yet I could see the country on every side. Eastward the City of Colorado Springs lay not very far away, beyond it the "plains" extended for miles an unbroken prairie without anything in sight, except the smoke of many railroad trains passing to and from the cities of Denver and Pueblo. Southward, nearly one hundred miles off, the Spanish peaks shone like shafts of polished marble. West of these the Greenhorn range joined the Sangre de Christo and the serrated backbone of the latter faded out of sight in the direction of Mexico. At our feet snugly nestled in the lee of Cameron's Cone the little village of Manitou shone as bright as if it were already Sunday morning. All at once it occurred to me that these things could not be seen in the night, and then looking upward I saw seven suns shining in the heavens; six of them were arranged in a circle around the seventh, which outshone the others more than a thousand times. It was a splendid array and I said:

"Flex, what constellation is now in sight?"

"It is the heavenly galaxy," he replied; "the central orb is Salem; the others are the primary planets that revolve around it; our sun is one of them; would you like to examine them?" he added, handing me the telescope.

Never again shall I see such a change as took place when I looked through that instrument. The great central orb and the suns surrounding it had lost their brilliancy, yet their beauty had increased more than a hundred fold. Each member of the galaxy was provided with a system of planets, the axes of the former standing nearly parallel to those of the latter.

Some of the planets were at perihelion and some at aphelion, and hence they extended outwardly in a curved line from the equators of their respective suns like balls of burnished silver strung on a segment.

"Look at Salem," said Flex.

At this time Salem filled the whole firmament, and we were apparently drawing nearer and nearer to it. My enthusiasm ran high ; I said to myself, "only one more stretch of power and I shall see its towers, and battlements, perhaps the pearly gates." Its beauty went beyond all description ; as it drew still nearer I saw a rainbow spring from its north pole and circling over and beyond the galaxy, it seemingly inclosed an area greater than the universe, and then completing the circle at Salem's south pole it stood there a circumambient flood of glory.

In following the course of the bow I thought I noticed Saturn apparently very close to the sun, and

I was about to remark: when Flex spoke more peremptorily than I had ever heard him.

"Keep your eyes on Salem."

Then I noticed a movement high up in the bow; apparently a glitter of working tools, and I imagined that I could distinguish the outlines of several persons, but they were so much within the body of the bow I could not determine what they were doing, yet I thought they were pitching a tent. Presently one of them came to the inner brink, and stood there plainly in sight. He was apparently a master workman clothed in shining garments; I saw him turn and look toward Salem. Oh, such a loving look. Then he scanned the bow upward and downward, at the same time smiling confidently, I thought almost contemptuously. Then standing erect he cast a plumb-line and the lead ran out for a thousand years swifter than a ray of light. And when he had calculated his countenance fell, and I heard one ask, "What is the measure of the arc thereof?" And the workman answered, "I cannot tell; the line is too short; the segment yields no sine."

I was very greatly astonished and I said:

"Flex, who are these people and what are they doing?"

"They are some of the inhabitants of Salem," he

replied, " out on a holiday, and one of them has undertaken to measure its first circuit and he has failed."

" Who is he that cast the line and made the calculation ?"

" That is Hiram," he answered, " Grand master of the workmen who builded the Temple at Jerusalem."

I was more than ever astonished and I said, " Is Salem's first circuit infinite ?"

He hesitated a moment and then replied :

" It *is* infinite in the sense in which the earth's is infinite, but the grand master was not trying to measure the infinite expression but the circuit which you saw."

Then as we drew nearer and nearer we heard one of them praying in a very low beseeching voice, almost a whisper: " *Dear Lord send them a philosopher ; Endow him with wisdom and special powers of discernment; Furnish him with all the knowledge of the past and a large intuition of that which is to come ; Give him a diamond pen ; and when he comes to write commission him as thy servant, so that he may with one stroke forever finish the career of the fiery hypothesis.* " Flex and I added " Amen."

Then the galaxy commenced to swing, not in procession but all together in sweeping grandeur, with their planets moving in course, and all their comets blazing in their orbits. My enthusiasm would be repressed no longer; I said : '

"Flex, I have given up all idea of making my home in the sun. My very eyes have seen the New Jerusalem! I want to live in Salem."

"It is the city of our God," said he; "I thought that sometime you would fall in love with it. Maybe it will please you now to hear a description of it in the quaint words of an old author who also saw it many years ago.

> "Hierusalem my happy home,
> 　When shall I come to thee?
> When shall my sorrows have an end,
> 　Thy joyes when shall I see?

> "Noe dampish mist is seen in thee,
> 　Noe cold nor darksome night;
> There everie soule shines as the sunne,
> 　There God himselfe gives light.

> "Thy walks are made of precious stones,
> 　Thy bulwarks diamonds square;
> Thy gates are of right orient pearle,
> 　Exceeding rich and rare.

> "Thy turrettes and thy pinnacles
> 　With carbuncles doe shine;
> Thy verrie streets are paved with gould,
> 　Surpassing cleare and fine.

"Thy houses are of yvorie,
  Thy windows crystals cleare;
Thy tyles are made of beaten gould,
  O God! that I were there.

"Our sweete is mixt with bitter gaule,
  Our pleasure is but paine;
Our joyes scarce last the looking on
  Our sorrows still remain.

"But there they live in such delight,
  Such pleasure and such play;
As that to them a thousand years
  Doth seem as yesterday.

"Thy gardens and thy gallant walks
  Continually are greene;
There grow such sweets and pleasant flowers
  As nowhere else are seene.

"There trees forevermore beare fruit
  And evermore doe springe;
There evermore the angels sit.
  And evermore doe singe.

"Hierusalem my happy home!
  Would God I were in thee!
Would God my woes were at an end,
  Thy joyes that I might see."

My eyes were filled with tears.

After awhile I said: "Do you know the names of the suns that compose the galaxy?"

"I have never heard any names for them," he replied, "except those derived from the Latin numerals. Beginning with the one north of our sun, they are Unis, Duos, Trex, Quarto, Quinto;—Sun. You will notice," he added, "that as these suns move forward in their orbital revolutions, their planets are also carried forward with them so that the planetary orbits are not in the same place this year that they were in last year. Hence, if you make a chart of all the orbital revolutions made by the earth during the period of the sun's revolution around Salem, you will have a series of ellipses clipping into each other all the way around very much like a piece of geometric lathe work," Fig. 39.

Fig. 39.

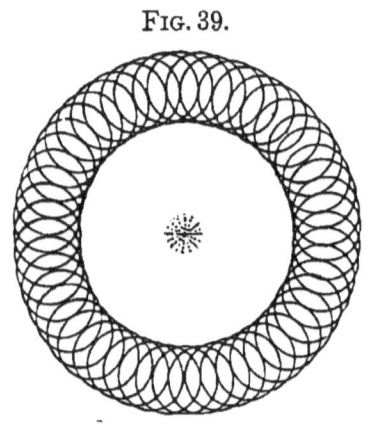

"Do you know the period of their revolution?" I asked.

"It is coincident with the precession of the equinoxes," he replied, "25,868 years."

Then the vision faded away, and with it the mountain, and we were again sitting in the library and I said : "Flex, there are many things about which I am greatly puzzled. I would like to know why some of the snow crystals do not conform to the general plan."

" You are laboring under a mistake," he replied. " You still keep thinking that earth, air, and water, are so essentially different from each other, that they may be entirely separated. You forget that a part of that which is air to-day may be water to-morrow, or indeed within a few minutes—and that a sediment will begin to settle as soon as the water is formed. When we see a mist rising from a pond, it is not merely vaporized water that is rising but air, earth, and water, and these quite frequently incorporated with noxious gases, and the bodies of living animalcules."

" And I also want to know why bees construct their cells so nearly in the shape of the molecules composing the air ?"

There was no answer, and so without knowing how or why, I began to think about bees.

Dr. Watts says :

> ''How doth the little busy bee
>    Improve each shining hour ;
> And gather honey all the day
>    From every opening flower.''

That is very prettily said, but there are some things

about a bee more wonderful than his industrious
habits or his honey. When he is abroad in the shining hours he is a laborer; when he is in his dark
home he is an architect busily engaged in making
cells, a great number of which are necessary to meet
the requirements of his household. Now this little
architect, in the dark and without any instruments
to measure angles, constructs these cells by hundreds
of thousands, all of them perfectly regular in size,
form and arrangement. Their shape is that of a
hexagon—that is to say a geometrical figure with six
equal sides and hence six equal angles. It is demonstrated in the science of mathematics that this figure
will fill any given space without interstitial loss of
room.

In order that the cells may be conveniently arranged and ventilated to meet his physical needs, he
attaches them to a partition. In doing this he uses
two angles, one of 70° 30′ and another of 109° 28′.
These angles are also the most economical that can be
used in such work. Having made these cells he
stores them with honey and other things, his pre-
cious property. From all of which it is obvious
that he is a laborer, an architect and a political econo-
mist. These three qualities are enough to make any
one worthy of great respect.

Now let us remember that his cells, like the snow crystals, have six points, and therefore every one of them is a picture of the magnetic force-lines found in the earth.

But here comes the architect; note him carefully! He plunges into the centre of one of the hexagons, and there with all his senses right at the whispering place, he is engaged in life work the sweetness of which fills the air all around. He is a masterpiece of workmanship worthy to be counted. *He is the seventh point.* On the other side of the partition there is an architect facing him but he knows nothing about that. The physical third circuit, *life,* is in their bodies. The mental third circuit is in their Creator.

Their big relative, the humble bee is the victim of a misnomer, besides being otherwise a very badly used personage. His name is *Bumble bee.* Nobody thinks of calling him anything else, except people who write books. He is a gentleman, almost too proud to work; I have known him ever since I was a child. Some years ago, he created such a stir among my associates that I was introduced to him more times than I cared to be. Such introductions are not particularly agreeable when ʼinsisted on from time to time. However, I have partaken of his hospitality and felt the warm shake of his —— I came very nearly saying hand. I know his reputation to be good ; so good that among the boys he needs no other defence than such as he is able to make for himself. I would not mention this were it not for the fact that I lately saw the following insinuation in one of the serials, perhaps the St. Nicholas.

> "Says the wicked flea to the bumble bee
>     You're a fat old meddling thing ;
> And if you will fight with me to-night,
>     Two pistols I will bring."

That challenge is an insult to a bumble bee. It must have been written by a girl ; no one who has ever crossed swords " for keeps " with a bumble bee would think of such a proposition. The bumble bee is not a coward nor a duellist, but a soldier and a terror. In the day of battle his courage is boundless. Like a furious Berserker,* sword in hand, or in tail,

---

* "A class of combatants among the early Norse people whose love of fighting led them to a fury of madness. They were so wild that chains could hardly restrain them. Friend or foe, bare breast or buckler, stick or stone, dead or living, all were the same to the Berserker when the fit was on, and he wandered aimlessly forth running an Indian muck at all he met. In later times the title was given to a company of hard fighters who were retained as body guards or special champions of renowned leaders. These periodical fits were

if you please, he rushes to the front and fights and fights and stings and stings; and dies a hero in defence of his home and property.

How many times we boys have been vanquished; how many times we have fled pell-mell from the field in utter dismay. Sometimes we were victorious, but not until the last defender was slain. Then we huddled around his demolished fortress and divided the spoils. There never was more than a cent's worth of honey all told, and the smallest boy usually got about a half cell of dirty looking yellowish gum, and with that he smacked his lips and was happier than any of us. I have not tasted bumble bee honey for more than forty years, but I am inclined to think that the idea of its excellency is a mere boyish fancy.

Now with these dead warriors lying all over the field, it is well to remember that every one of them was born in a somewhat slovenly constructed six-pointed cell, and that the same is true as to all their

---

called the 'Berserk's course' when under his mad influence the Berserker was a raging wolf to his friends and an armed maniac to his enemies. In the Yulinga saga we read, 'But his (Odin's) men rushed forward without mail, and were as mad as dogs and wolves, and bit on their shields and were as strong as bears and bulls. Men slew they and neither fire nor iron laid hold upon them.' "

forefathers, and although adverse circumstances have compelled them to follow the military profession, yet they also " improve the shining hours."

If we had leisure to examine the latest work on distant relationship, we would probably learn that honey bees and bumble bees are simply an example of abstemiousness in one case, and voracity in the other. No doubt a quotation from such a work would read about as follows : "Some very remote ancestor of the present bumble bee race happened to be unable or unwilling to control his appetite, and so got fatter and fatter, and at the same time more and more furious (which is not usually the case), and these characteristics transmitted in the descendant line through many generations caused the bee family to differentiate into two permanent types, the one a useful branch of society, the other such as has been described." Now in behalf of the bumble bee I ask permission to file his *general denial*, together with a true statement of his character. Nevertheless, if the aforesaid hypothesis can be reasonably applied to the whole animal creation, I will confess judgment for the bumble bee. But if he is to be made an exception, then I am retained and I will demand a jury trial.

Then I took up the three sections of the apple, and joining them together, I said to myself, " these pieces fit into each other like the joints in the backbone of an animal. More like that of a fish than that of a land animal. The middle section is almost perfect. The others rudimentary. Can it be possible that the vertebral bones of an animal took shape in some way similar to the manner in which the earth was constructed? Has magnetic force been tampering with the spinal column of an animal? Can I afford to admit that a living creature may be the effect of a physical force? *If I do I am lost!* What answer can I make when arraigned for my presumptuous temerity if I should be mistaken? I fitted the pieces together and nervously took them apart again. I was wide awake; no doubt of that, and therefore not to be excused as I might hope to be for the other night's work. *What answer can I make?*

Then I looked again at the magnetic frame, Fig. 16. "These lines," I said, "are the very lines on which the earth was built. I carved the apple with reference to *nothing whatever* except the magnetic forces, and these are the pieces. He who made the earth made the animals on the earth and in the water, and if I have any right to inquire how he made one of these things, I have the same right to inquire how he made the others."

There was a small shriveled lemon on the table.

14

"I will put you to a good use," I said, and suiting
the action to the words, I scored a line around it in
the neighborhood of its arctic circle, another at its
antarctic, then an ellipse on its surface to represent
about the depth the second circuit enters the earth,
that is to the fire-line. Then taking short pieces of
lead pencils, I stuck one into its north pole, and one
that had been sharpened at both ends into its south
pole. And one at each side of its arctic and antarctic
circles. Then setting it on the table I said to it: .

FIG. 40.

"Once you were a lemon and as
such you were of little consequence.
Now you are a turtle and still you
are a failure. But as an illustration of the magnetic forces, you are
a success. Your head is not by any
means equal to a problem in Euclid,
but it is the best one you ever had.
It is the place where the first circuit of magnetic force
entered your body, and whatever intellect you have is
due to that fact. Your head counts for one, Fig. 40.

"Your tail seems to be nothing more than an artistic
development; that is the place where the first circuit
left you, which was a very unfortunate circumstance,
for had it remained with you, you might at this moment be discussing the matter with me.

"Your fore and hind legs were developed by the force of the second circuit. They are in fact *your northern and southern auroræ.* The only trouble with you is that when the first circuit left you, your development ceased. If I knew for what cause it left you, I would tell you, but I do not. However, I have the honor to inform you that you score six points, and if you were a living specimen that fact would make seven. And now since I have spoken rather disparagingly of your tail, I will also inform you that the antarctic regions of your great proto-type, the earth, are in about the same lamentable condition.* I hope both of you will come out all right."

Another look at the diagram, Fig. 16, carried my

* "The two polar regions differ greatly. The seas of the arctic teem with animal life. Land animals, such as the bear, wolf, reindeer, musk-ox, and arctic fox, are scattered over the frozen surface of the land where they find the means of sustenance. The air is peopled with innumerable flocks of birds, a hardy vegetation extends close up to the arctic circle and beyond it, mosses, lichens, scurvy grass, sorrel, small stunted shrubs, dwarfed trees, and in summer beauti-ful flowers. In the antarctic, on the contrary, vegetation ceases at a certain limit, trees terminating at about 56° S. latitude. Animal life abounds in the seas, but though birds exist in great numbers and in varieties unknown in the

thoughts back to Pennsylvania, as it was more than forty years ago. I remembered the condition of its wood-land counties at that time; the slaughter of the wild animals, large and small, and this brought to my mind the shapes of every variety of hides and pelts, which were then nailed to the barn doors. "Here," I said, "is the sum of the whole matter; every creature of the higher order has been formed on the same general plan, and mankind may have been included."

Then there arose a great clamor of voices and wide-spread indignation prevailed. Every voice seemed filled with a full circuit of wrath as it fiercely demanded: "*Will you dare to apply your sacrilegious philosophy to the body of a living man?*"

I answered firmly, "*I intend to do it.* I have been commissioned to inquire into this matter. As prosecuting attorney for the Commonwealth, I brought a turtle to the bar and made him answer for his points. I will not be a respecter of persons. Nevertheless, in deference to public opinion, I will not press this

---

arctic, no quadrupeds are found upon the land."—Johnson's *Cyclopædia*, article Polar Research.

Sir Joseph Hooker says : "Geographically speaking there is no antarctic flora except a few lichens and sea-weeds." —*Nature*, London, 1881, p. 447.

prosecution further than one example. But whether he be a king or a philosopher, he shall come into court and answer as to the points of his entrance. *Mr. Sheriff, bring in a man.*"

There was a bustle in court. A couple of important looking personages seemed just then to have urgent business with the sheriff. Presently a young man about twenty-five years of age took his place on the stand. Waiting a moment for his embarrassment to subside, I said : " What is your name ?"

" Aw weally !" he replied, " Dontcher know Chawles Augustus Sidney Algernon—aw—De Smith ?" I was provoked and I said with some severity :

" State to the jury ; are you a citizen of the United States ?"

" Aw weally !"

" Answer the question ; do you vote ?"

" My deah boy ! Dontcher know—aw—fellah cawnt mingle with the—aw—*beastly men ?*"

" Who created you ?" I demanded more fiercely than such a question should be. " Answer promptly or I will speak to the judge and he will commit you."

" Aw weally ! Oi used to think that, dontcher know—aw God, beg pawdon, had a hawnd in it, but of late years—weally, bah jove oi have some doubts."

One of the jurymen winced and I looked toward the bench, but the judge was apparently asleep. "You may take the witness," I said.

Then opposing counsel bade the witness "stand aside," and turning to me said: " We will offer no testimony in this case but rely wholly on the record."

Then I realized that the case was desperate, yet I replied: " The State will waive the opening, you may go to the jury."

Then senior counsel for the defense rose and addressing the court and jury said : " The issues to be tried in this case may be briefly stated as follows: Was man created by the same physical force that created the beasts ? Was physical force involved in the creation of either ? Does man bear the impress of magnetic force on his person ? The last inquiry is in the nature of testimony, but we deny that such testimony exists, and hence, its existence or non existence forms one of the issues in the case.

" In order that you may have a complete understanding of the various matters to be tried, we will first state the theory of the plaintiff.

" He maintains that there are three circuits of magnetic force. That they are life circuits. That they have existed in all past time, and will continue to exist during an endless future. That the first circuit enters the body of every creature, from the least insect to the largest beast. That the force of the second circuit adds to this life the capacity for physical development. That the third circuit is in some way connected or correlated with immortality, but in what manner is not clearly set forth in his pleadings. That owing to malformation or some other cause (here again he is very vague), the third circuit never enters the body of any creature except a man. And notwithstanding this admission which we think is clearly contradictory to his own theory, he urges that man bears the very stamp of his conjectured dynamics.

"He will endeavor to make you believe that the molecules of the air and water are imbued with magnetic force. That when we drink our stomachs extract this life principle from the water and send it through our systems. That in breathing the air we have another connection with his supposed circuits. The only difference that he will admit is that which exists between the organs of our bodies and a possibility that there is less of this vital force in one of the elements than in the other.

"From his written pleadings we are unable to determine in what manner a man is connected with his third circuit, but as we have no idea that he will be able to impress your minds with that part of his theory we will not dwell on it.

"He will tell you that when the earth was young, there was only one circuit in powerful action, at least so far as it was concerned. That it was then covered with water; that shortly afterward a second circuit entered the field, and that all the creatures that then sprang into life had a close connection with the first circuit and a very slight one with the second, and that there is testimony of this stamped upon their anatomies. That as the waters gradually subsided the sway of the second circuit gradually increased causing the creatures that sprang into life later to exhibit more plainly the impress of both circuits. That all this resulted from the fact that two circuits of magnetic force were approaching each other.

"And then as a cap-stone to his whole theory he claims that when the two circuits effected an union, the third circuit entered the body of a man, and in that circumstance, he urges, lies the only difference between him and a beast.

"Having heard the whole case, it will be obvious to you, that his theory is based on nothing except a chain of analogies not one of which is supported by anything except his *ipse dixit.* For this reason we have appeared in the case not to try the issues of law and fact, but to see that no errors occur in any of the proceedings. Trusting to your intelligence and the solid position each of you occupy in society we have no doubt you will render your verdict in accordance with the public will." Then pausing a moment he added, "*vox populi vox dei.*"

Then I addressed the court and jury and said:

"We are laboring under some disadvantages in endeavoring to present this case. One of which results from an apparent conflict between the documentary evidence* and the scientific testimony. The court will instruct you to consider both and we hope you will give the whole subject your earnest attention, and that you will find that no such conflict exists.

There is another matter of still greater importance, and hence much more embarrassing to our case. It lies in the fact that the relationship existing between the Creator and the creature is susceptible of demonstration, but unfortunately the witness who appeared, had no knowledge of the fact.

We do not claim that the learned counsel for the defense has unfairly presented our theory, and yet a subject of so much importance cannot be stated in a

---

* The Holy Bible.

few brief sentences. Hence we ask you to compare his remarks with our pleadings and the record, and if he has unwittingly misconstrued us, ascribe to us only the theory set forth in our pleadings.

In order that you may know how I came to be of counsel in this case, I will state that some years ago I undertook an examination of magnetic force. I may say that I thoroughly investigated the subject in the light of the ablest scientific works then to be obtained, and finally *in manner and form* as the same appears in our pleadings, I came to the conclusion that He who created the forces of nature and established all their resultant phenomena is not a respecter of persons or things, that is to say, He shows no partiality to this or that, man or beast. Then turning to the documentary evidence I found it written that not a sparrow falls to the ground without His notice. And that He also hears the young ravens when they cry for food.

Strengthened by this testimony I thought I would apply magnetic force to men and things with such impartiality as I might be able to exert.

First making the application to the earth I found that two circuits of magnetic force enter its body. Coming to examine the scientific witnesses one of them testified that he had found a third circuit flow-

ing from east to west.* Other witnesses slightly cor-
roborated him. Pushing my investigations further
I found the impress of the first two circuits stamped
upon it, but the impress of the third circuit seemed
to be wanting. However, I accepted the testimony
of the witnesses, and constructed the theory set forth
in chapter three of our pleadings. And now in cor-
roboration of that theory we will call your attention
to the documentary evidence, we read :

In the beginning God created the heavens and the earth.

2. And the earth was without form and void; and darkness was upon the face of the deep. And the spirit of God
moved upon the face of the waters.

3. And God said, Let there be light ; and there was light.

4. And God saw the light that *it was* good : and God divided the light from the darkness.

5. And God called the light Day, and the darkness he
called Night. And the evening and the morning were the
first day.

If you will compare what took place in this first
period with the theory advanced in chapter three of
our pleadings, you will find no conflict whatever, not
even in the minutest detail.

The first two verses refer to the time when the
solar nebula was about to become a separate system.

---

* André Marie Ampéré.

The words " *without form and void*," mean that the forces had not yet formed any nucleus or solid matter. That the place which the earth was about to occupy, was empty of anything that can produce phenomena. You will notice that darkness was the condition of interstellar space, and that it was " *the spirit of God*" that moved upon the *face of the waters* (primordial matter), and the latter immediately began to aggregate at or near the places now occupied by the members of the solar system. At the command of its Creator, primordial matter began to flow toward the hitherto empty place, thus forming the nucleus of the earth. At the same time the disengaged gaseous matter surrounded the nucleus forming an atmosphere, and of course luminous phenomena were the inevitable result followed by other phenomena.

And God divided the light from the darkness. That is to say, interstellar space still remained dark just as it is now, the light being confined to the atmosphere surrounding the earth's nucleus.

We trust you will not be mistaken. It was the spirit of God moving upon the waters. *Fire is not mentioned, nor intense heat,* but water, which is the reverse.

The earth may not have been larger than an asteroid at that time, but it was there, and this fact closes the first period.

The sun may not have been larger than the moon is now, and it may have been so enveloped in primordial matter that no relation existed between it and the earth, perhaps not even between it and Mercury.

Evidently the next step in creation is the continued growth of these bodies, and the consequent clarification of the spaces around each of them. However, the documentary evidence describes only the earth. We read :

6. And God said, Let there be a firmament in the midst of the waters, and let it divide the waters from the waters.

7. And God made the firmament, and divided the waters which were under the firmanent from the waters which were above the firmament; and it was so.

8. And God called the firmament Heaven. And the evening and the morning were the second day.

Again, compare this with our pleadings, and we think you will agree that the firmament so established, included a space sufficiently cleared of primordial matter, to permit the moon, or at least the effects of it to be noticeable on the earth. If this be so, then the second period closes with the earth in binary relation with the moon, and hence three powerful circuits in the field.

We are about to read the result of this, or rather the beginning of the result, for we ask you to particularly notice that first results are not as great, or at least not so impressive as those which occur later in the same period, and this you will find applies to all the periods.

9. And God said, Let the waters under the heaven be gathered together unto one place, and let the dry land appear; and it was so.

10. And God called the dry land earth, and the gathering together of the waters called he seas; and God saw that it was good.

That is the history of the early part of the third period, and it is still water that is being divided; moreover, it is always in the plural. Evidently the source of the inspiration was not contemplating water in mass as we contemplate it, but was regarding *the individual atoms or molecules which compose it.*

You may carefully look over this evidence and you will not find a word or a hint, indicating that the earth had been hot and was cooling down. The idea that it ever was intensely heated *is false.* It has been derived from the fact that vibrations have always tended toward the centre of the earth causing intense heat in certain localities. And in times past and even at present, inward disturbances have and still are throwing portions of the earth's interior to its surface. From this and a superficial examination of the subject, certain persons who were not familiar with the documentary evidence were led to think that the whole earth was once a ball of fire. It was a very foolish conclusion, and we earnestly hope you will not believe it.

We will now read what took place when the earthly lunar binary relationship reached the zenith of its power.

11. And God said, Let the earth bring forth grass, the herb yielding seed, and the fruit tree yielding fruit after his kind, whose seed is in itself, upon the earth : and it was so.

12. And the earth brought forth grass, and herb yielding seed after his kind, and the tree yielding fruit, whose seed was in itself after his kind; and God saw that it was good.

13. And the evening and the morning were the third day.

The moon is only 240,000 miles from the earth. A binary relation with it constituted three very powerful circuits, and they were life circuits,—*living vegetation with seeds and fruit.* You will also notice that the grass came first, the herb next, and later in the period the tree yielding fruit. Moreover, the source of this inspiration does not apply the contemptuous pronoun *it* to these things, but exalts them with *"his,"* using the male pronoun in its generic sense.

What a wonderful transformation from a sandy,

stony world to one with grass and fruits, and flowers, for while the latter are not mentioned they undoubtedly preceded the fruit.

We can form but little idea of the luxuriant vegetation resulting from such close magnetic relationship. But if you will reflect on the density of the aqueous atmosphere surrounding both bodies at the time referred to, and the coal formations which took place thereafter, you will gain some knowledge of the power of the lunar-earthly circuits.

Three days are gone, God's days. Do not forget that in every instance the evening is the beginning of the day. The fourth day is at hand. We read:

14. And God said, Let there be lights in the firmament of heaven to divide the day from the night; and let them be for signs, and for seasons, and for days and for years.

15. And let them be for lights in the firmament of the heaven to give light upon the earth; and it was so.

16. And God made two great lights; the greater light to rule the day, and the lesser light to rule the night; he made the stars also.

17. And God set them in the firmament of the heaven to give light upon the earth.

18. And to rule over the day and over the night, and to divide the light from the darkness; and God saw that it was good.

19. And the evening and the morning were the fourth day.

The sun is 92,000,000 miles from the earth. During the first day in which God's spirit moved upon the waters, the sun also became a solid body of matter with an atmosphere surrounding it. "His tabernacle was set in the heavens." During the second day the firmament surrounding him extended outwardly and he secured a binary relation with Mercury. On the third day he embraced Venus. Now it is the earth's turn, and here comes another life messenger, one of God's servants; *on time.* His circuits are sweeping the universe; the solar nebula is clarified by them. The *moon takes a subordinate position; the stars appear.* This is an evening piece. In the morning he will kiss the misty mountain tops of the earth; drink the dew of its valleys; and then throwing showers of kisses back at them, he will descend and clasp the ocean in his arms, and all the waters of the earth; and in his tender loving embrace the real work of the fifth day will begin. We read:

20. And God said, Let the waters bring forth abundantly, the moving creature that hath life, and fowl that may fly above the earth in the open firmament of heaven.

21. And God created great whales and every living creature that moveth, which the waters brought forth abundantly, after their kind, and every winged fowl after his kind; and God saw that it was good.

22. And God blessed them, saying, Be fruitful, and

multiply, and fill the waters in the seas, and let fowl multiply in the earth.

23. And the evening and the morning were the fifth day.

And God blessed them. Perhaps there were responsibilities connected with his blessing such as we know nothing of. At all events it is the "*fittest*" of them that have survived till now, and the departure of these from the original stock may have been in some cases so wide that we cannot distinguish any family resemblance.

Let not the greatness of these events distract your minds from a consideration of the time in which they occurred; the half days begin to count. What a mighty day's work that was! What will the sixth day bring? We read:

24. And God said, Let the earth bring forth the living creature after his kind, cattle and creeping thing, and beast of the earth after his kind; and it was so.

25. And God made the beast of the earth after his kind, and cattle after their kind, and everything that creepeth upon the earth after his kind; and God saw that it was good.

It is now noon of the sixth day. To-night the physical forces of God will finish their work. There is now every creature, our minds can conceive except one. There are those that must live in the water, and those that must live on the land, and some of

them can live in either element. There are those
that live on the land and fly in the air, and also those
that live in the water and fly in the air. And yet
there are none that can live in the interstellar spaces.
No creature that can soar through infinite space and
admire the works of his Creator. But there is an
afternoon yet. Oh, what mighty events may take
place in an afternoon! Surely this afternoon we
shall see a creature who may disregard heat and cold,
light and darkness, and all other phenomenal conditions, and determine by personal investigation many
of the questions which so puzzle our minds. We read:

26. And God said, Let us make man in our image,
after our likeness; and let them have dominion over the
fish of the sea, and over the fowl of the air, and over the
cattle, and over all the earth, and over every creeping thing
that creepeth upon the earth.

27. So God created man in his own image, in the image
of God created he him; male and female created he them.

28. And God blessed them, and God said unto them. Be
fruitful, and multiply and replenish the earth and subdue
it; and have dominion over the fish of the sea, and over
the fowl of the air, and over every living thing that
moveth upon the earth.

We are contemplating the close of the sixth day
and the beginning of the seventh. Is creation finished?
It is not so stated. But man has been made ruler

over all the earth, and the controller of his own destiny. This delegated supremacy makes him the representative of God, *i.e.*, " *in the image of his creator.*"

And God blessed them just as he did the creatures of the fifth day and he also gave them the same injunction.

And now this new king who is in the image of his Sovereign will ascend the throne in the morning. Meanwhile let us examine his pedigree.

In this connection, we will enumerate for your consideration the universal physical forces of God in their cosmological order.

Attraction and Repulsion.

Motion and Rest.

Heat and Cold.

Light and Darkness.

Noise and Silence.

Life and Death.

Ease and Pain.

LOWER OCTAVE.

The following is their dynamic arrangement.

Attraction and Repulsion. Motion and Rest.

Heat and Cold. Light and Darkness. Noise and Silence.

Life and Death. Ease and Pain.

Heat and Cold. Light and Darkness. Noise and Silence.

Attraction and Repulsion. Motion and Rest.

As you will observe life and death ; plant life, and ease and pain; animal life, are the effects of the third circuit.

These are the forces that have been at work in God's direction, and the result of their six days' work is animal life. Such forces are not competent to make the creature we have in contemplation. Yet from them sprang the man who is to have dominion over the earth and himself in the morning. We read :

1. Thus the heavens and the earth were finished, and all the host of them.

2. And on the seventh day God ended his work which he had made ; and he rested on the seventh day from all his work which he had made.

3. And God blessed the seventh day and sanctified it ; because that on it he had rested from all his work which God created and made.

Is creation finished ? It is not so stated. It is the heavens and the earth and all the host of them which are finished. The six days are gone, and the physical forces have ended their work.

Let us contemplate the condition of the earth at the close of the sixth day. The shells and bones of the inhabitants of the fifth day lay in heaps. Nay more, in geological strata from the mountain tops to the fire line. Every one of these shells had been a part of a living creature, not one of which died without God's notice. On the coast of Florida there are quarries wholly composed of shells cemented together by the petrified juices of the creatures that once occupied them.

Let a small boy write a line of figures and keep adding ciphers to the right of it until he has reached his three score and ten years, and then he may not have expressed the number of creatures that died before the lowest form of intellectuality entered the earth. God knows the number of them. He blessed every one of them long before it lived. He knows what it cost to make a physical man. He also knows that many of them are not worth it.

But we are at the beginning of the seventh day. And man is to take charge of affairs. Look out for wild work! The six days' conflict of the opposing physical forces that made the earth and peopled it, are gone. The tremendous battle of contending mental forces is at hand. The creature that is to occupy the interstellar spaces, comes to-day or never. Do not be discouraged, God has blessed his servants and sanctified the day of battle. It is to be a success. By Monday morning, perhaps to-night, there will be a creature able to surmount an inter-

stellar chasm, such as Herschel never dreamed of.
Has God abandoned the world? Not yet. Now he
breathes into man's nostrils the breath of life. That
is to say, he places the mental forces fully under his
control. And now God rests.

What are these forces? The following are the
mental forces arranged in the order of their creative
and destructive scientific sequences.

Instinct or Reason.

Love or Hate.

Good or Evil.

Faith or Despair.

The Holy Spirit or Evil possession.

Joy or Misery.

Immortality or Death.

MIDDLE OCTAVE.

The following is their dynamic arrangement.

*Instinct or Reason. Love or Hate.*

*Good or Evil. Faith or Despair. Joy or Misery.*

*The Holy Spirit, or Evil possession. Immortality or Death.*

*Good or Evil. Faith or Despair. Joy or Misery.*

*Instinct or Reason. Love or Hate.*

You will observe first, that these forces are not directly creative or destructive of physical life, yet
when considered in their dynamic arrangement, the
first series uniformly tend to lengthen it, while the

second series tend to shorten it. You will also notice that instinct or reason, the first expression, may be connected with either love or hate, or good or evil, the second expressions. And a very thoughtful consideration of the whole series leads to the conclusion that there is a gracious connection all the way through this octave. Even the depths of despair and misery, may lead to an acceptance of the Holy Spirit, and the change so brought about will re-establish the preservative series. Yet as you can not fail to notice when studying the dynamic arrangement of the forces, the connection between the destructive series and the preservative series becomes very faint after entering the third circuit.

Moreover, we desire you to notice that the Holy Spirit and evil possession, immortality and death, are the alternate effects of the third circuit, and that these important possibilities are located at the whispering place.

The third circuit is the most occult force in nature, both in the physical and in the mental octave. Because in the former it is the highest and lowest expression of physical force; *life* and *death*. In the latter it is the highest and lowest expression of mental force. *Immortality* and *death*.

The lower octave is the dividing line between matter and mind. The middle octave is the dividing line between intellectuality and spirituality. These two octaves comprise all the sciences of earth, and the latter leads to and includes the first branch in the sciences of heaven.

You may think it strange that we should classify the emotions and arrange them as a part of the science of dynamics, but why not? Are they not the greatest power on earth? Are they not also from the same source?

We want you to know that if anything at all is the effect of force then everything is. We want to impress your minds with the fact that our faculties spring directly from our physical organizations, and the latter from the forces of God which we are considering, and therefore they must be the counterpart of the forces from which they came.

We want you to cease thinking, *I am a man, you are a worm,* therefore, I possess that which you do not possess. We beg you to remember that God is not a respecter of persons. That in his mind an advancing progressive race of oysters is of more value than a degenerating retrogressive race of men. We want you not only to understand, but to realize that the mental forces are not in your exclusive possession. Sea crabs get fiercely angry when tormented, and a

worthless cur will love you so much that you will
weep over his dead body.

You must realize that the gentle sunshine and the
dreadful earthquake are the handmaidens of God
engaged in creative work, such as we are not yet able
to comprehend.

If you are ready to believe in the *" survival of the
fittest,"* and apply it to the lower octave, then carry
it through the middle octave and on to the upper
octave, and you will find your feet planted on the
rock of everlasting truth. *It is undoubtedly the fittest
who will survive.*

Some of these thoughts may be new to you; so
much the more reason you should study them. God
may never take the supremacy from the human race,
but he is able to do it, and that too without perform-
ing any greater miracle than we see every day. That
he does not do it, is because the race, as a whole, still
deserves the highest rank. Fair play yields no other
reason. Whenever the forces of evil begin to domi-
nate the earth, the covenant of supremacy on our
part will be broken ; the doom of the race sealed.
God's sentence and the execution thereof will go
hand in hand, creation will still proceed without in-
terruption. There may be wild work in the morning
of the upper octave and yet the fairest of days ensue.

But the seventh day is here and man is king. Oh, there was wilder work this morning when the first note of the middle octave sounded than there had ever been on this earth. Think of men whose highest faculties were love and hate. Think of the sweet love of a mother and the fierce hatred of a savage. How often has the babe been torn from its mother's breast and dashed to death in her presence? *Love and hate!* Who would have thought that the gentle influence of the former would ever hold its own against the hellish power of the latter? Yet out of that deadly conflict came the knowledge that love was always right and hate forever wrong. We do not care to dwell on these sequences; they are too plain to need it.

Now before we close this branch of our subject, we want to call your special attention to the words, "*the evening and the morning,*" as they appear in the documents. You will observe that it is difficult to follow days which are described in this way. We seem as we read to drift into the idea that each day should begin in the morning and end that same evening. This is not the case. If you thoroughly examine the evidence and carefully study our pleadings, you will understand that the work of each day really began the preceding evening, and this is precisely what

would be the order of action with a continuous progressive movement under way. For instance, it is
not likely in a constantly developing creation, that a
single day or year could be selected when the moon
lost its supremacy, and the sun began to rule over
day and night. Neither could any single moment,
day, or year, be selected when there was a fauna on
earth possessed of life, and hence, subject to death,
and yet no individual member of it capable of ex-
periencing any higher sensation than ease and pain.
Necessarily some of them would be more and some
less advanced.

Again, it is not likely that at any given time in
the early part of the seventh day all men were possessed of the faculty, love and hate and nothing
higher. Take men as they are to-day, some are
more advanced than others. Some have loving dis-
positions and these recognize that good is good, and
try to regulate their conduct in accordance with this
conviction ; they are apt to soon have faith in God
and the Holy Spirit communes with them. While
there are men who hate and prefer to hate, these recognize evil and yet continue to do it. After awhile
they despair and then misery and evil possession fills
their souls, and mental death is awaiting them ; some
of them recognize this fact, but blindly ascribe this

same end to the whole race and with this comfortless fallacy appear to be satisfied.

Again, studying the lower octave we find it to be a scientific fact that the solar nebula had been separated (not fully so, for that is not the case now), from the other nebulæ in the same circuit prior to the morning of the first day. That separation was the work of the preceding evening, and it is a suggestion of the creator of nebulæ. Almighty God.

Therefore in cosmological order the evening of the first day was the commencement of the second. The spacious neighborhood of the earth began to be clarified by central aggregation. At the close of the second day the moon was in sight, but its beams met nothing but the wild sweep of a tempestuous ocean.

The evening of the second day was the commencement of the third, the magnetic power of the moon began to gather the water into seas; later the dry land appeared and at the close of the third day plant life was on the earth perhaps only grass but still living vegetation.

The evening of the third day was the commencement of the fourth. There was already life on the earth; plant life, trees, and fruit, things able to distinguish the "*signs*," *i.e.*, heat from cold, day from night, the coming fall and returning spring. Meanwhile the circuits of the sun were bridging the mighty chasm between it and the earth. The power of the moon was diminishing. By the close of the fourth day the sun and planets were in sight and the second order of sublunary affairs established.

The evening of the fourth day was the commencement of the fifth ; vegetation was engaged in producing food; then a creature existed capable of distinguishing ease from pain and therefore especially worthy of God's notice. This creature may have been almost a plant; it was of the water; more than likely it was not capable of moving from place to place; possibly it drifted with the element in which it lived. But whatever may have been its estate, it is certain that it was the first scientific life effect of the approaching power of the sun. Later in the day the monsters of the ocean appeared and at the close of it all the waters of the earth teemed with life and the air was filled with aquatic fowls. And God blessed all of them from the least to the greatest.

The evening of the fifth day was the commencement of the sixth. The ocean was shrinking, the area of land enlarging. Later in the day the bayous and shallow lagoons were drained ; the land was producing less wood and more fruit, perhaps not more abundantly but in greater variety. By noon the

fructifying influence of the sun had peopled the earth
with four-footed beasts and creeping things. At the
close of the day men and women stood upon the earth
and looked upward toward heaven and we believe
toward their God.

The evening of the sixth day was the commencement of the seventh. Men and women were on the
earth admiring what had been done. Naming things,
that is to say, constructing a language. And God
continued strengthening their minds. Breathing
into them the intellectuality, impliedly promised
them, thus making them capable of having dominion over the things which he had created. And
in the morning of the seventh day men had all the
mental forces at their command, and God commissioned them, and said to them: If you want to be
nearer to me? If you want to learn of infinite things
and their relationship? If you desire immortality
and free scope? *Then know* that I exist and comprehend both good and evil, love and hate, joy and
misery, heaven and hell. And I am Lord over all.
And I desire you to live in the enjoyment of my
life-giving series by conquering death's destructive
forces and *trampling them under your feet.* This you
are able to do.—This you must do or I will cut you
off from the glorious knowledge of my universe.

Yet I know your feeble estate, and therefore I have left an umbilical cord attached to you. It is as strong as the freedom necessary in soul creation will permit. It is enough, and you will find it growing stronger and stronger as long as you regard my admonition. You have my blessing.

Then men took charge and immediately began to construct their own theories, some of them very foolish ones.

If the six days' work of creation seems a complicated subject when presented in connection with the physical forces of God, when shall we have sufficient intellect to set opposite to each of these forces its subordinate phenomena, of the first order, and of the second order, and so on? From attraction and repulsion spring galvanism, molecular attraction, atomic repulsion, chemical affinity, life, and sexual relationship, and the mental forces follow.

To contemplate a series of such forces is the work of an immortal soul, and that is the principal thing the whole series, both physical and mental, are engaged in creating at the present time.

But the defendants claim that men were immortal ever since they were created, and that the *specimen* who was on the stand is one of these immortal souls by the power of God heretofore exerted.

Their attorney has not seen fit to offer their theory, but says he will rely on the weakness of ours.

Gentlemen of the jury, our theory as compared with theirs, is a bulwark of truth. But it is not only our theory that is on trial, but theirs also.

What is their theory? We will now set before you what the defendants are pleased to call the " forces of nature."

*Original Impulse.*—An imaginary something that in past time shot the worlds into space in a right line.

*Attraction of Gravity.*—A disposition the aforesaid worlds have to fall into each other on account of their weight.

*Centrifugal Force.*—A tendency they have to do the opposite thing to that last mentioned.

*Light and Heat.*—Derived from the sun either directly or indirectly. Created by combustion, or friction, or shrinkage in mass.

*Darkness.*—Absence of light.

*Cold.*—Absence of heat.

*Life.*—Animated existence. In man immortality. In the beasts transient life.

*Death.*—A transition in man from one state of existence to another. In the beasts, annihilation, or oblivion.

16

This ramshackle theory the defendants expect you to sustain by your verdict. In accordance with their theory, immortality was created by the physical forces.

If that is true we ask you in the name of reason, what was the need of the battle of the seventh day? Why should God rest, while man had control of some of the most dangerous powers? Why should blood and tears enough have been shed to water the earth? Why should hate, evil, despair, misery, evil possession and death have existed? In such case there was no work for them to do except devils' work.

If their theory were true, then the alternative mental forces would be a reproach to God. According to our theory, they are the crucible from which souls of pure gold flow, and the dross is returned to the earth from whence it came.

Their theory means that God breathed the spirit of life into the nostrils of men on the sixth day instead of the seventh. It means also that he breathed the most excellent thing our minds can conceive into men filled with hate. It denies that God's spirit, the Holy Spirit is a sequence of faith. It ignores the fact that God is breathing his spirit into his servants on the field of battle. He is not resting, according to their theory, but has abandoned the world ; or that it came by chance, or that it was the creator of itself in some inexplicable manner. In fact it is a denial of God himself and a substitution of *" original impulse,"* and many of the defendants not being able to maintain this conclusion in reason and logic have by the near cut placed themselves on a platform of general denial.

We do not care to argue it further. There is not one of the physical or mental forces recognized by them, that can be made the sequence of another, without arranging them as we have arranged them. And when this is done, immortality goes to the head of the mental series, and immediately it becomes a suggestion of the upper octave—Almighty God. And when an individual recognizes this, he is no longer a defendant in this case, but a soldier of the cross fighting for his own immortality and the redemption of the world.

There is another matter needs explanation ; you will remember that there was a fauna created on the fifth day, and as the fifth day began on the evening of the fourth, this was a very old fauna. The development of its individual members had been under way all through the thousands of years comprising the fifth day. By the afternoon of the sixth day the

most advanced race of them may have reached a state
high enough for them to recognize love and hate,
good and evil. This race would be the masters of
the old fauna just as mankind became the masters of
the new; they were probably moon worshipers.
Their ancestors had seen the time when the moon out-
ranked the sun; they may not have been pleased
with the new order of things; they had sprung from
the water and yet probably had become able to live
on the land. This old master race were in the midst
of the garden, that is to say they possessed the highest
civilization then on the earth, or at least the nearest
approach to civilization. They were the rulers of the
world and this excited the admiration of the new
race.

Now these old serpents, for so they have been denominated, were probably schooled in iniquity. Such
iniquity as their race had invented and improved
during thousands of years. And very soon after the
advent of the new race they were found tampering
with the sources of life and death. In other words,
seducing mankind from the path of virtue and mor-
ality. No doubt they tried to think that their ways
and the ways of their people were all right; they
were audacious enough to say that no penalty would
follow a violation of the commandments of their God

and our God. Nay, more, they insisted that sin was a pleasant thing to indulge in and would be beneficial to the new race, and when the measure of their iniquity was full, the sentence of the Lord God went forth, and the serpent race staggered under it and their degeneration and retrogression began.

Is he a dirt eater? If a lineal descendant of one of you jurymen should at some future time find himself in the condition the serpent is now in, and could recognize the exalted position held by you, his ancestor, he would think himself humbled to the very dust.

Did he walk erect? It is not so stated. However, he is possessed of six anatomical points. No doubt when his sentence was pronounced, jealousy and hatred of the new and advancing race (for so it is stated) filled his whole being, and these faculties predominating for a great length of time, changed the course of his physical and mental life from advancement to retrogression, and finally these accursed forces settled in his head, giving him a pair of fangs and a couple of sacks of poison to correspond. Such a result is in strict conformity with the latest ideas on evolution, and a survival of the fittest. With this difference, that it is an example of degeneration and a survival of the infamous.

We have noticed this circumstance in early history,

not because it falls strictly within our case, but because an attempt has been made with it to discredit the documentary evidence on which we rely.

There is another series of forces strictly within the case at bar. The organized forces. These, have in a certain sense, accomplished more good, and also more evil, than the individual forces. Their power lies in the average development of their component parts. Yet occasionally extreme ideas prevail, often for good, sometimes for evil. The following are the religions God has recognized in the order in which they have dominated the world.

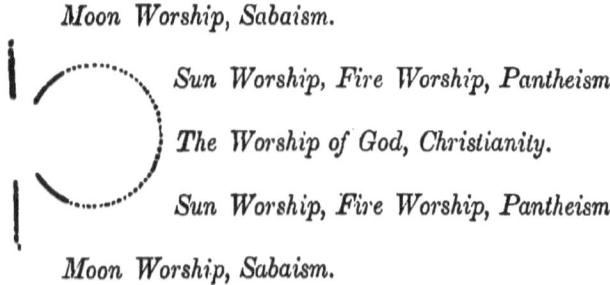

*Moon Worship, Sabaism.*

*Sun Worship, Fire Worship, Pantheism.*

*The Worship of God, Christianity.*

*Sun Worship, Fire Worship, Pantheism.*

*Moon Worship, Sabaism.*

This series comprises the parent stock of all religious thought from the beginning to the present time.

We would not be presumptuous in matters of this kind, yet we believe, there never has been a church organization under any of the above forms, which did not at some period of its existence contain members who looked beyond its forms and ceremonies up to the living Creator of the universe, and therefore received his blessing. We hesitate more to say, and yet we will say, that we believe that a compliance with the forms and ceremonies of such church, whatsoever they may have been, were beneficial to its members so long as they knew no better way.

The forces mentioned in this series have, of course, lapped backward and forward as the other forces have done.

The serpent race were moon worshipers. The earliest offspring of mankind were also moon worshipers. Cain "offered the fruits of the ground," emblematic of the power of the moon, or rather the power it had had in olden times. Abel offered a living sacrifice emblematic of the power of the sun. The stronger current of inspiration was with the new dispensation. The older organization was more powerful in numbers. A religious conflict arose, the moon worshipers prevailed. Abel was slain. He was a martyr to the advance of religious thought. Finally the new dispensation was victorious. Then the devotees of the old faith expected to be annihilated. God said: Nay!—He had long before that prescribed what should be the punishment for adhering to false religious ideas and their adjunct, sin. He had placed a mark upon the serpent race, and he now places a mark upon Cain. That is to say, retrogression, and all that it implies began. The very countenances of the adherents of the lower faith became different from those of the higher faith. The mark was one that all might see ; and therefore Cain and the moon worshipers emigrated from the presence of those who were outstripping them in life's battles. They went east to the land of Nod. Literally nobody cared where. Yet there is no doubt that many of them afterward accepted the new religion.

From this first religious war came the old adage, " They shall surely ask counsel at Abel."* That is to say, if you are in doubt on any subject of importance; if you have a disagreement with your neighbor ; in short, if you want knowledge of what is right and what is wrong, inquire of those who worship God. Such an inquiry saved Cain and his people from destruction. It has also saved a remnant of the Indian race, and at the same time given them more than they deserve. The voice of God's people has always been the voice of a powerful and merciful umpirage.

" They shall surely ask counsel at Abel." If the most excellent members of the Christian Church are

---

* Second Samuel, 20–18.

not inspired, then they are deprived of that which
God's people have had ever since the beginning of
the world. If the Christian Church were at this
time asked, What disposition shall be made of the
liquor traffic? the answer would well up from the
ministry of the smallest denomination and down from
the church at Rome, and all Israel would re-echo the
words, "*Let it be forever outlawed.*" And they would
now have the power to demand it had they not in
times past been guilty of the intolerance condemned
by God in the example of Cain and Abel.—Religion
is an individual responsibility. Intolerance is high
treason to God's government, and since his people
were convicted of it, he has divided them. Nay,
their own crime divided them ; therefore we see them
standing at the polls distrusting each other, and all
of them appalled at the work accomplished by the
united cohorts of rum. Christians should stand side
by side. What right has the man who is working in
God's vineyard with a gang plow to find fault with
the man who is using a hoe? how much less right to
ask whether he intends to dine on white or black
bread. He should be glad that he is in the vineyard,
and exceedingly thankful that both of them are provided with food.—God will know when the time
comes in which his people will be able to govern the

world, and at the same time abstain from persecuting others on account of their religious belief, and when it does come, they will be given the control. He has promised that his saints shall take the kingdom and possess it forever; not those who simply adhere to some particular form of worship, but *His saints.* The promises of God do not relate to some other world, but to this world. They are to be fulfilled here; right here while the righteous and the wicked dwell together, and the latter are to have the full benefit of the good government the former will institute.

This cannot be the case so long as there is a trace of intolerance in the minds of his people.

God no more intends that the righteous shall persecute the wicked than he intends the reverse of it. He has prescribed the punishment for sin and for unbelief. He has delegated no authority to his church or to his people in that respect. If any of the members of his real church ever did lend assistance to the punishment of those who differed with them, they were apostates at the time and worthy of great condemnation. Some of them had the same stripes, torture and death at the stake meted to them. Whatever may be the opinion of others, we cannot think that high treason ever went unpunished.

However, these wretched years are gone, and it seems to us that there is a spirit beginning to prevail in the minds of men, clearly indicating that the time is not very distant when the government will be in the hands of God's people. Indeed, we think it is now, to as full an extent as they are worthy of it.

We are not mistaken as to the significance of this old adage. " They shall surely ask counsel at Abel." It was brought to light in one of the cities named by the old Canaanitish sun-worshipers. Doubtless named after the first martyr of their church. A woman made it the preface to an appeal for the life of a city. Women are very apt to remember church lore. The appeal was successful, but not until the head of the offending party was thrown over the wall.

Balaam was a prophet of God ; his integrity was too strong to be shaken by any bribes or so-called presents that a king could offer. Yet he was a Canaanite, his name implies a priest of Baal,—a sun-worshiper ; that he got angry and would have killed his ass if he had possessed a sword is simply an exhibition of human nature. He was long afterward slaughtered by the Jews who were at that time God's executioners.

The religious struggle in Abraham's mind was

whether to continue in sun-worship or break away from it. His early education and religious belief led him to offer his own son as a sacrifice. Baal worshipers considered this the supreme offering; it would have been more than this in Abraham's case, for Isaac was the prop of his declining years. His newer inspiration was not to do it; his faith consisted in the fact that he was ready to do either as God would direct. The new light,—the newer inspiration prevailed, wherefore God promised to be his shield and his exceeding great reward.

Moses had his conflict with fire-worship in the edge of the desert at the base of Mount Horeb. His mighty mind was able to pierce through the fire, the emblem of God, to God himself; his soul was happy; he considered the ground where the conflict took place as holy ground. He took the shoes off his feet, and then and there God commissioned him and never afterward forsook him.

These are some of faith's old conflicts; we have ours. Shall we anchor ourselves to the letter and to the emblems, or shall we rise to a comprehension of the power of God as manifested in his forces and in his works.

Melchizedek, the man who fed Abraham and his people when they were returning from a successful

military expedition, was king of Salem then a
Canaanitish city. Abraham paid him one-tenth of
the spoils of war as an acknowledgement of his kingly
authority; Melchizedek was also a priest, as nearly
all kings were in those days. No doubt the ceremonies of his ordination were performed by a priest of
Baal; yet he was also a priest of the most high God.
*The ancestry of God's real priesthood is without be-
ginning and its lineage without end;* hence his priesthood has not been confined within the limits of any
particular forms or ceremonies. Abraham, who had
been a sun-worshiper himself, acknowledged this
fact by receiving his blessing.*

This incident occurred several hundred years before God sentenced the sun-worshiping Sodomitish
Canaanites. One cannot read the passage without
being impressed with the idea that it once contained
a fuller account of what took place. And one can
almost *feel* the reason why it is not there now. After

---

* There is nothing to warrant the conclusion that King
Melchizedek was anything more than a true believer, an
honest hospitable priest and king. St. Paul's comments on
the passage were intended to convince the Hebrews that
God's real priests were not exclusively of the sons of Levi,
nor "after the order of Aaron," but "after the power of
an endless life."

sun worship had led to the most infamous practices, and God had condemned it and sent forth the Jews as his executioners, it was hard for them to believe that their father, Abraham, had acknowledged a priest of Baal to be a priest of the most high God. Indeed, at several periods in their history it would have been their ruin had they so understood it. But that time is past both with them and us; we are not slaves delivered out of Egypt, and ready to run after any god, even a calf. The trouble with us is, that we are not willing to acknowledge the true God, or admit that he has any priesthood on the earth.

One evening while passing through a forest in Africa, I came to a very shady place where the trees stood thick, and their branches extended so that they interlocked each other and almost shut out the light of day. It was a very lonesome, secluded place. Presently I saw a black man some little distance off, he was not aware of my presence. As I came nearer to him I observed him stoop over and gaze intently on something which appeared to be the bone of some small animal. I could see his lips move and there was a very earnest expression on his countenance; in a few minutes he laid himself down and pressed his face to the earth. I was almost ashamed to be secretly watching him, for I knew that he was engaged in worship. Then he rose and I could see a gladsome look on his face as he passed into the forest. I said to myself, " That man has acknowledged his weakness and asked aid of the only God he knows; I believe he has been benefited.'' And then and there my heart acknowledged him as a member of the church militant.

What part did magnetic force bear in the creation of man ? The same part it bore in the creation of beasts. When we consider it in the light of its apparently infinite manifestations, we find no reason to deny that it is one of the powers of God existing in all material things. And further that He is above and beyond it, farther than it is above and beyond our comprehension. But in order to realize this, we must divest our minds of every prejudice. Nay more, we must pass our hearts through the crucible, time and again, until every vestige of partiality and superstition is smelted out of them, and then we shall be able to contemplate God's works as *His works,* whether the same be a force, a crystal, an insect, or a man. Yet long before this takes place, we may be able to view this subject as the Psalmist did. We read, 139th Psalm.

14. I will praise thee; for I am fearfully and wonderfully made ; marvelous are thy works ; and that my soul knoweth right well.

15. My substance was not hid from thee, when I was made in secret, and curiously wrought in the lowest parts of the earth.

16. Thine eyes did see my substance, yet being unperfect; and in thy book all my members were written, which in continuance were fashioned, when as yet there was none of them.

Evidently the Psalmist saw by inspiration the limbs of a man extending by the force of the second circuit. He realized that the work had been done in a *secret place.* That both the place and the curious development that performed the feat were hidden from him and from mankind. Undoubtedly, the forces of God were endeavoring to explain to him a scientific fact. He so understood it. He knew that it was knowledge, great knowledge, which was being presented to his mind. Alas! He also knew that he was unable to comprehend it. He said:

6. *Such* knowledge is too wonderful for me; it is high, I cannot attain unto it.

How could these things take place in the "*lowest parts of the earth?*" For an answer to this you are referred to our pleadings, where you will find that the earth aggregated in a *cool* deliberate manner. No doubt this proceeded while men went through all the stages mentioned by the Psalmist. The Psalmist was looking backward to circumstances which occurred thousands of years before. He was capable of receiving the grandest thoughts that faith can inspire, but a clear, cold, scientific fact was too much for him. He was a shepherd boy in his youth, and for this, and a still greater reason, he was not permitted to enjoy the dearest wish of his heart. To erect a temple to his God.

We would have you read the whole Psalm. No matter if you have read it a hundred times. It is worthy of many more readings. He was contemplating the ways of God toward men with a degree of fervor, perhaps never equalled. Why should he not at such a time be inspired with knowledge unknown to men?

"*In continuance.*" From when to when? From the time when man's members were yet only in the mind of his Creator, to the time when a lineal descendant of the man-like stock of the sixth period, should in the seventh possess the condition that would enable him on the subsequent morning to enjoy an universe of worlds. The man who wrote the Psalm is doubtless one of these, notwithstanding his great transgression. We would have you consider the age in which he lived, and the condition of his fellow-men; his fellow-kings. if you please, and

17

then render your verdict whether he was inspired at the time he wrote the 139th Psalm.

If the elucidation is not clear enough to suit you, extend to him the favor you would ask if you were endeavoring to explain a scientific thesis too difficult for your own comprehension, and infinitely above the minds of your readers.

There is another question involved in this case. It is the central point of the main issue. Is the human race endowed with immortality? Or is there only an opportunity offered to its individual members to attain unto it.

We placed a witness on the stand, or rather the defendants selected one for us. Had they brought in such a man as we wanted, he would have testified in your presence as to the time and place, at which, and in which, the spirit of God entered his heart. He would have explained to you the method of its operation more clearly than you will ever have magnetic force explained to you. Had they brought in a stalwart specimen of their forces, he would have impressed your minds with the fact that the sweetness of the third circuit had never yet entered his mortal body. And a rigid cross-examination of him might have revealed the presence of death's forces. In short they were caught between the premise and conclusion of an old-fashioned syllogism, and therefore, they brought in a *fellow*, such as in old times, when plain language prevailed, would have been called a fool. We disclaim the witness.

However, you have seen him on the stand. His anatomy shows five points; his life counts for six. If you think yourselves justified in considering his reason superior to that of a beast, it makes seven; that is the number the four-footed beasts have. There is not a suggestion of the upper octave on the person or in the character of the witness.

In bringing such a witness, they mistake the forces that are arrayed against them. Their brief is too brief to meet and counteract the eternal forces and effects that are engaged in creating immortal souls. We ask you whether that man is fit to roam at large in the universe? Is he the perfected work of the forces we have enumerated? Is he an immortal soul? Will he be commissioned in the morning and sent back to earth to help redeem its people? Or will he be found squat at the whispering place, suggesting to some poor troubled soul, " *Now you are old enough to have some doubts.*" This is the nature of his effeminate life work. Will he be permitted to continue it indefinitely? Is his life so important that his evil influence cannot be got rid of? We know that God

was able to make a man who would be mortal or immortal according to his desert; is it not safe to conclude that that is what he did do? We ask you to
look at the witness; is he a fair representative of the
sturdy old father who accumulated the wealth he
now revels in? Do you not discover that retrogression has already begun? That he has started in the
path of the old serpent race? Will the result be the
same or will God be a respecter of persons? Shall
the *"survival of the fittest"* prevail in the physical
octave, and the fit and unfit both survive in the mental octave?

It is written that the wages of sin is death; that
the gift of God is eternal life and that the gift is for
them that love Him and keep His commandments.
What will be the state of those who do not is a
question in many minds. We think it is plainly answered in the documents. The answer is *death;* we
think it means mental death; we may be mistaken,
we hope we are; we most earnestly hope it does not
mean oblivion. But suppose it does, what a dreadful thought for a creature that has enjoyed life to
contemplate? *Life,* which after all is nothing more
than a realization and enjoyment of the good things
of this earth. Think of these things when you are
considering what your verdict shall be. Think of

the enjoyment you have had here, and then think of
the universe of worlds which you know exists; think
of the mighty events of the past as they are set forth
in the documents and in the record; think of the infinite regions of space where similar events may now
be transpiring. And then ask yourselves this question : *Dare I come to the conclusion that I am an immortal soul, without more evidence of the fact than the
testimony of witnesses ?*

Gentlemen of the jury, we will now comment on
the last and *best evidence* bearing on the case and then
we will close."

Here the judge seemed to be laboring under some
misunderstanding, for he placed the jury in charge
of the sheriff, and before I could make an objection
they filed out to consider of their verdict.

Then feeling greatly depressed, I bowed my head
and thought. How foolish of me to rely on a single
witness when I might have called others; I lamented
the unfaithfulness of the sheriff; the apparent indif-
ference of the court and jury. And, as I reflected on
the great issues involved in the case and the labor I
had bestowed upon it, there came to my mind the
many, many times, I had imagined this the trial-day,
and that I had made a masterly effort, and that the
jury had given me their verdict. O, how different

the reality ! The trial finished. The case lost. *Lost!*
*Lost for the want of testimony?* with all the earth, air
and sky teeming with evidence. O! that the greatness of a great issue should be belittled by the
weakness of its advocate. O! the blindness of over
confidence.

Then the whole scene faded from sense and memory,
and there was nothing in sight but a wilderness of
black sage and sand. It seemed to me that I had
travelled a long journey, and that I had not seen a
road or pathway for many days. Then weary and
lame, and disheartened, I thought of retracing my
steps, but that seemed impossible ; night was coming
on and I was lost. Just as I thought to give up, lay
down and die, I saw a rock some distance ahead,
and taking courage, I dragged myself to it, and
climbed to the top. There was nothing in sight but
the trackless wilderness. Nothing to indicate that
any one had ever came that way. " This is a wilderness without end," I said. " Here my journey ends."
Then I recalled the events of a long life, and bitterly
repented my misspent days, and made vows for the
future, and laid down under the protection of the
rock and slept,—and dreamed. It seemed to me that
I was again in the library, and that my wife stood
looking over my shoulder at the confusion of things

on the table, and that my youngest son stood on the other side admiring the figure of the turtle. And I was happy, and I placed an arm around the boy as my wife said :

" What in the world have you been doing ?" And I answered, " I have been trying to write my idea of the three circuits."

" Is that you, and I, and Walter?" she asked.

" Not by any means," I replied. " But as sure as fate, we three are representatives of their best earthly expression."

" What have you been doing ?" I said. " We have been measuring for a new carpet."

" How many yards is it likely to take ?" I asked with some concern.

" Forty-two," she replied.

Then it seemed to me that the scene shifted, and that the court had been in session a full term, and was about to close " without day." That the journal entries were being signed by the judge, and the record made up. Presently, I heard one attorney speak to another in a low voice and ask, " What entry is to be made in the case of the *Commonwealth against a philosopher ?*" Then it came to my mind that I had been disbarred for some misdoing in term, and that a motion for a new trial had been considered by the court and overruled, and that my counsel had informed me that there was " no error " in any of the proceedings, and " no appeal." Then I realized the hopelessness of my condition. That I was ruined;—irretrievably ruined. And it seemed to me that I prayed as I never had done before. "O God is there any power in Heaven or on earth able to wipe out the infamous record of my guilt?" Just as my anguish became greater than I could bear, a young man rose and addressing the court said:

"The defendant in this case is a friend of mine. I ask permission to examine the papers before his sentence is pronounced;" O, how hopeless his effort seemed. O, how well I knew that able counsel had not left a line or word in any of the papers unchallenged.

Then it appeared to me that I was asleep under the edge of a rock in the wilderness, and that a heavy hand was placed on my shoulder and that an authoritative voice said: " *Idle dreamer, awake! Stand up like a man, and answer me as to the points of your existence: I am the Lord your God:—All that you are, or ever have been you owe to me ; I created you out of the dust of the ground ; and yet all the best years of your life have been spent in disregarding my precepts, and in breaking my commandments; besides*

*boasting of your infidelity to the church of my people,
you have ridiculed my servants, and tried to seduce
my ministers; I have forgiven you; now will you serve
me the remainder of your days or shall I cut you off?"*

I could make no answer; I crouched into the very
cleft of the rock exclaiming, "Lord Jesus, help me
or I will perish?"

Then a gentle hand was placed in mine and I distinctly heard the words: "Fear not! I will be with
you always, even unto the end of the world."

I arose and the desert had passed away and the
sun shone on tree and flower, but the rock was still
there and at its base flowed the mightiest river I had
ever seen, and as I uncovered to enjoy the refreshing
breeze that wafted from its surface I saw Flex
standing by my side; grasping his hand I said,
"What great river is this? It seems to be endless."

"*It is the river of life,*" he replied, "*that flows hard
by the throne of God.*"

Then we both knelt down and drank,—a soul sat-
isfying draught. Then seating ourselves under the
shade of a linden tree we talked about the old times
in Kansas. Of the troubles we had there; the great
hail storm, and the grasshopper raid; of the buffalo
and their extinction. The great plains and the gal-

lant struggle under way to reclaim them. As we talked the other side of the river seemed to draw nearer and nearer until we heard a voice saying: " Dear Lord, there are two servants of thine seated on the other bank, and one of them has patiently led the other all through his wayward life and now they are both ready to enter here; shall we go and welcome them."

"Not yet," was the reply, "but you may give them our blessing." And we heard the words of it.

" The grace of the Lord Jesus Christ and the love of God, and the communion of the Holy Spirit *be* with you all: Amen." And we also responded, " Amen."

After which we spent a few minutes in thinking of the deep things which had been revealed to us. Then I said, " Flex, I am filled with joy and hope and confidence. It seems to me that I love the Lord with an all-conquering death-defying love: *Can this be science?"*

" *It is the semitone of God's love,"* he answered, " *the highest science in the universe.*"

Then I sat down at my own table to write the eighth chapter of this work. I am not weary but refreshed. O how gladly I cross the line that divides the last earthly science, from the first heavenly science: O for power to write the possibilities of an octave the first note of which is immortality.

"Free grace and dying love."

I heard the bells of a thousand towers proclaiming.

"*Free grace and dying love.*"

And as I cast my eyes toward heaven, and toward God, the universal upper octave sounded from Salem to the earth.

"*Free grace and dying love,*
*O ring those charming bells.*"

"Lord Jesus! I am ready; commission me now to write the glories of thy everlasting kingdom."

"*You are not to write it!*"

"O, gracious Lord! I have set my heart upon it!"

"*You are not able to write it; the honor of reconciling the sciences of earth, with the sciences of heaven, is reserved for my servants, priests, and ministers.*"

"O, my master! O, my Lord! Am I not a servant of thine?"

"*Thou art a servant of mine.*"

"Dear Lord it is enough; I serve. Let me take my place among them that watch and pray!"

"Lead kindly Light! amid the encircling gloom
    Lead thou me on ;
The night is dark and I am far from home ;
    Lead thou me on ;
Keep thou my feet : I do not ask to see
The distant scene : one step enough for me.

" I was not ever thus, nor prayed that thou
    Shouldst lead me on ;
I loved to choose and see my path ; but now
    Lead thou me on ;
I loved the garish day and spite of fears
Pride ruled my will, remember not past years.

" So long thy power hast blest me, sure it still
    Will lead me on
O'er moor and fen, o'er crag and torrent till
    The night is gone ;
And with the morn those angel faces smile
Which I have loved long since, and lost awhile. "